Books by Candace Shaw

Harlequin Kimani Romance
Her Perfect Candidate

CANDACE SHAW

was born and raised under the sunny skies of northwest Florida and knew she wanted to become a writer after reading *Little Women* in fourth grade. After graduating from the University of West Florida with a degree in elementary education, Candace began teaching and put her dream of becoming a writer on hold until one summer vacation she started writing again and hasn't stopped.

When Candace is not writing or researching for a book, she's reading, shopping, learning how to cook a new dish or spending time with her loving husband and their loyal, overprotective Weimaraner, Ali. Candace is currently working on her next fun, flirty and sexy romance novel.

You can contact Candace on her website, at www.candaceshaw.net; on Facebook, at www.facebook.com/AuthorCandaceShaw; or tweet her, at www.twitter.com/Candace_Shaw.

Her PERFECT CANDIDATE

CANDACE SHAW

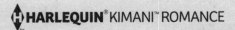

HARLEQUIN® KIMANI™ ROMANCE

For my girlfriends Brenda, Kenyatta, Lisa, Mary and Tonya for their love and support as I embark on this new chapter in my life.

For my husband, Bobby. Where would I be without you? Love you!

Recycling programs
for this product may
not exist in your area.

ISBN-13: 978-0-373-86360-0

HER PERFECT CANDIDATE

Copyright © 2014 by Carmen S. Jones

Printed in U.S.A.

www.Harlequin.com

Dear Reader,

The idea to write *Her Perfect Candidate* came about from watching decorating shows on HGTV and listening to a certain U.S. senator from Illinois speak at the Democratic Convention. What I didn't know was that years later he would be the president!

Megan Chase is ambitious and goal-oriented with her main focus on her career, even though her friends keep setting her up on boring blind dates. But when she meets charismatic and sinfully irresistible Steven Monroe, she can't shake him from her thoughts.

With his smooth talking and sexy smile, Steven is a ladies' man who has no intentions of changing his philandering ways. But there's something about Megan's bubbly and whimsical personality that has him wanting to win more than just the election.

I hope you enjoy reading Megan and Steven's journey of winning each other's hearts. Feel free to contact me at www.candaceshaw.net.

Sincerely,

Candace Shaw

A big thank you to my girls, authors Sharon C. Cooper and Delaney Diamond. I'm so happy we are on this journey together. Charlie's Angels for life!

Chapter 1

"Great!"

Megan Chase plopped her forehead on the steering wheel. It was early evening in rush hour traffic, and her SUV had just gotten a flat tire on Interstate 85 in Atlanta. Luckily, she was in the far right lane and was able to inch the vehicle over to the shoulder. She lifted her head, breathed deeply and eased open the door to survey the damage. But before her 4-inch heel could hit the pavement, she quickly drew it back in observing the cars zooming by at high speeds.

Shutting the door, she moved her laptop bag and purse from the passenger seat into the back, before climbing over the gearshift. The flat was on the back passenger side. She figured she could change it and then be on her way to meet her twin sister and her best friend at a scholarship fund-raiser event one of her clients had invited them to.

She hopped out of the SUV and walked carefully along the rocky pavement.

"Of all the days to dress up," she said, pulling her short black dress down to barely touch her knees. She stooped down to look at the damaged tire. The tires were new, so she wasn't quite sure why she had a flat. A nail, probably, she thought.

Earlier that day, she'd put the finishing touches on decorating a model home in a new subdivision outside of Atlanta. Houses were in the process of being built, and Megan had toured the subdivision to see the homes. She figured she'd run over a nail in the process.

As she popped the trunk to retrieve the tire, she heard her cell phone blaring from her purse in the backseat. Climbing through the trunk of her SUV to reach the phone, she knew who was calling before she even looked at the display. Now, glancing down at the caller ID to confirm her suspicion, she saw Sydney Chase's name flash on the screen. Megan knew if she didn't answer the phone, Sydney the worrier, would probably have the FBI, CIA and the SWAT team scouring the city for her within the hour.

The sound of a horn and tires on the gravel behind Megan stopped her from answering the call. She grabbed the mace she always carried in her purse and began to climb backward out of the SUV. Her finger placed firmly on the spray button.

As she turned around to step down, a fine-looking

tall man was standing in front of her opened trunk, with his hand out to assist her. She blinked twice and stifled a "Goodness he's gorgeous" with a slight gulp. The sun was going down behind him radiating an aura of bright yellow and orange.

"Need some assistance, pretty lady?" the sexy, baritone voice offered.

Megan tossed the mace spray over the backseat and placed her empty hand in his. His touch on her skin, although brief, sent a warm shiver through her veins. Once settled onto the pavement, she squinted her eyes and placed her right hand straight across her forehead to see him better without being blinded by what was left of the sun.

She looked up in amazement at the most handsome man she had ever laid her eyes upon. He was quite tall, at least a few inches over six feet. His hair was neatly trimmed with black wavy ripples. The evening sun was bringing out the color of his smooth, milk chocolate skin, and she fought back the urge to run a hand over his hairless, chiseled face. He had thick eyelashes that supermodels would give up purging their dinner for. His charming smile displayed pearl-colored teeth between his inviting lips. While he had let go of her hand, she could still feel the warmth of it on her skin. She wondered how his strong hands would feel on the rest of her body.

For a moment time stood still. She didn't notice the cars zooming by them or the April sun bearing down on her. Instead, she thought about how he reminded her of the man she always dreamed about.

The man who would one day rescue her on his white horse and love her forever.

Suddenly remembering that he'd asked her a question, she blinked several times before coming down from cloud nine.

"Do I know you?" she asked, studying his captivating face.

A delicious grin crossed his mouth causing her to almost sigh out loud. *Stay composed, girl. You see handsome men all the time.*

"I don't think so. I would definitely remember you if we knew each other," the sinfully sexy gentleman stated in a tone that caused another wave of heat to rage through her.

What the heck is wrong with me?

"Oh, sorry for staring so hard, but you look familiar," Megan replied, studying his face carefully. Megan wasn't good with names, but she never forgot a face, especially one as intriguing as his. She couldn't help but stare at the yummy dimple on his right cheek that appeared every time he smiled.

"What's your name?" Megan asked.

"Steven."

"Nice to meet you. I'm Megan."

"Do you need some help changing that tire?" he asked, nodding his head in the direction of the flat. "It's too dangerous for you to be out here alone."

"Oh, yes. I…" she stuttered, glancing toward the tire. *This man is making me forget why I'm standing out here in the hot sun in the first place.* "I was just about to change it."

His left eyebrow rose. "Really?" His gaze traveled the length of her body. "Wearing Louboutins and a very…um…sexy little freak'um dress. Are you trying to cause accidents? Seeing you bent over trying to change a flat tire will cause a ten car pileup," he teased, taking off his blue suit jacket along with a red tie and handing them to her. "I'll take care of it, while you call back whoever keeps calling you." He nodded down to the cell phone in her hand that kept vibrating. "Your man is probably worried."

She shook her head and glanced at the caller ID. "It's my sister. We're supposed to meet for an event…" She stopped to glance at her watch. "I'm thirty minutes late and big sis is concerned," she said, watching Steven take the spare tire and jack out of her trunk. He then slammed it shut and turned to look at her.

"I completely understand. My brother is always checking on me and he's younger. How many years apart are you?"

"Two minutes," she answered. "We're twins."

"So there are two of you?" A cocky grin formed on his lips. "Nice," he commented, barely loud enough for her to hear as he rolled the spare tire over to the flat one. "You're more than welcome to sit in my SUV and wait. The sun is going down, but it's still hot. Crank the ignition and turn up the air conditioner if you'd like."

Megan looked past him at the white Range Rover. *He seems like the type to own such an elite SUV. Tai-*

lored business suit, expensive watch and a powerful, masculine presence.

"Thank you. I'll call my sister and let her know I'm fine." She walked steadily on the gravel toward the passenger side of his Range Rover. Once settled in the plush leather seat, she cranked the car as he suggested and was pleasantly surprised to hear Sade singing "Smooth Operator" through the speakers. She turned the volume down when she saw the light flash on her cell phone again.

"Hello?"

"Megan, where are you? I've called you like five times!" Sydney exclaimed.

"Syd, I'm sorry. I had a flat tire, but I'll be along soon," Megan answered quickly. She was too busy gazing at the jaw-dropping man who was now peeling off his dress shirt to reveal a white undershirt. The shirt did little to hide the gorgeous muscles of his arms, chest and back. A thin sheen of sweat glistened on his forehead. *He looks so damn hot and fine.* Megan reached over and turned the air conditioner to full blast.

"Are you listening?" Sydney asked in an impatient manner.

Who could listen at a time like this?

"Huh? What did you say?"

"I said do you need any help? Or are you changing it yourself?"

"No, this kind man is changing it for me." Megan continued to watch as Steven lifted the flat tire off, showcasing the toned muscles of his arms. *Oh, my goodness!*

"Kind man? You mean strange man! Where are you?"

"Calm down, Agent Chase. I'm sitting in his Range Rover watching him change my tire. He's almost done," Megan said, a little disappointed. "Poor thing, he's sweating. I think I have some bottled water still left in my lunch cooler. Syd, this man is so gorgeous!"

"Um…is this the same Megan that swore off *all* men almost two years ago when her ex-boyfriend cheated?"

"I didn't swear off all men, I just said I needed a break from dating and that mostly included all of the blind dates you, Jade and Tiffani had been arranging for me. I don't have a problem being single." She frowned as Steven replaced the last lug nut. He looked up and flashed a million-dollar smile, causing her to suck in her breath and become slightly turned on.

"He's done. I'll see you in a few." Megan abruptly hung up the phone to avoid any lectures from her sister about being safe. Sydney was a criminal profiler with the Georgia Bureau of Investigations, and in her book, everyone was a suspect.

Megan hopped out of the passenger seat and walked over to Steven who was wiping the sweat off of his forehead with his dress shirt.

"You're going to ruin that shirt," she said, opening the back door of her SUV and reaching over to pull out a small, unopened bottle of water from a small ice cooler. She opened the cap and handed him the water.

"Thank you, pretty lady." He gulped down half of the bottle before taking a breathing break and then downed the rest of the water. "The shirt will be fine. I'm headed home to change clothes anyway."

Megan watched him intently as she thought of something else to say. She knew in a minute they'd be back in their own vehicles, going back to their already scheduled day. She didn't notice a wedding ring—just a college ring. But that didn't mean he wasn't seeing someone.

"Thank you so much for changing my tire for me. I must've run over a nail today while driving around a subdivision's construction site."

"Having a home built?"

"No. I'm an interior decorator. I just finished a project in one of the model homes and decided to drive around the subdivision." She hoped to find some way to keep the conversation going, but he was already buttoning his shirt and checking his Rolex. She decided not to delay him any longer. He needed to go, and she needed to leave as well before Syd assumed she'd been kidnapped.

He stepped toward her as she closed the back door. She leaned against the SUV as he stood directly in front of her, literally in her personal space. The woodsy scent of his cologne swirled in her nose, sending tingles through her body. *I wonder what his scent would smell like intertwined with mine?*

Her lips parted slightly as he stared down at her, she thought surely he was undressing her with his eyes as they raked over her.

"Thank you again. I hope I didn't inconvenience you, Steven."

"No, not at all. I'm very glad I pulled over to help you," he stated in a sincere tone, running his eyes over her body one more time before they settled back on her face.

She smiled up at him before stepping over to the passenger door. He opened it for her and she slid in, crossing her legs and turning her body to face him.

"Bye, Megan," he said hesitantly before shutting the door. He gave her one last smile before strolling back to his car, whistling.

Steven watched as the loveliest vision he'd ever laid his eyes on drove away. When he first saw her in the trunk bending over the backseat of her Acura MDX reaching for something, he couldn't help but wonder if her toned caramel-coated legs and thighs matched the rest of her. The way her little black dress hugged her bottom and hips as it rose up, stirred his manhood. He had decided to take a chance. Plus, he couldn't possibly leave a female on the side of the highway with a flat tire.

Her long, curly brown hair with subtle blond highlights flowed down her provocative bare back in an utterly sexy manner. He would've given anything to run his fingers through her soft curls, or better yet, spread them out on his pillow as he looked down at her.

He'd been pleasantly surprised when she turned around to acknowledge him. Strikingly stunning, she had a pleasant smile, high cheekbones and wore very little makeup. Her almond-shaped eyes were cinnamon in hue and when he stared into them, he felt a sense of overwhelming peace.

Steven admired all women, but Megan stirred feelings and emotions he'd never felt before in the thirty-three years of his life. Her pleasant personality and warm demeanor were a breath of fresh air.

While changing the flat tire, he couldn't get the image of Megan's short black dress and shapely legs in black heels out of his head. He had let his eyes roam all over her breathtaking body while he tried to make polite conversation. It was hard to do, considering she had the perfect hourglass figure. Her perky, rounded breasts and small waist were followed by hips that settled snuggly but tastefully in the dress she wore.

He had tried to move his eyes back up to hers so she wouldn't realize he was checking her out, but instead they'd rested on her inviting lips. Sexy, luscious lips painted in a reddish shade that he enjoyed watching move. He didn't care what she was saying, he just wanted to devour them. He felt a rise in his briefs again as he thought about the possibility of being kissed by the sexy interior decorator.

He didn't mean to step into her personal space, but he'd needed to see her supple lips up close once more.

It took everything he had in him not to drag her body close to his and kiss her senseless right there against her SUV. The way he noticed her checking him out as well, he wouldn't have been surprised if she had responded. However, he was shocked at his thought. Kissing was something he didn't do. Sex, yes. Kissing, no. It was too emotional, and he wasn't looking for an emotional relationship with anyone. Yet, kissing the beautiful Megan was all he could think about.

As he drove toward his penthouse in Midtown, it dawned on him that she didn't recognize him as the Georgia state senator Steven Monroe, son of Robert Monroe, United States senator. Coming from three generations of politicians and Harvard Law School graduates, the Monroe family were considered to be the black Kennedys because of their millions, power and influence in the political world. Because of who he was, most women usually flirted with him and did any and everything possible to garner his attention.

Steven leaned his head back on his seat and inhaled the sweet scent of the intoxicating perfume lingering in his SUV. *Damn, why on earth didn't I ask for her phone number?*

Megan searched through her console between the seats for her Sade CD with her right hand as she kept her left hand steady on the wheel. She needed to hear "Smooth Operator" one more time as thoughts of Steven filled her head. She was surprised at her thoughts but couldn't help but smile. She then glanced at herself in the rearview mirror to see how she looked when he met her. Upon finding the CD, she slid it into the CD player and waited anxiously while it loaded. She skipped the first few songs until she heard the beat of "Smooth Operator" and turned the volume up.

As she was singing the song for the second time, she saw Syd's cell number flash on the dash. She had the Bluetooth hands-free function connected to her car, which made it safer for her to talk to clients while driving. She turned off the music and pushed the cell button on her steering wheel.

"I'm almost there, Syd," Megan said as she exited the interstate. She then turned toward Atlantic Station, an outdoor mall in Midtown Atlanta that housed the swanky hotel Twelve, where the fundraiser gala was being held.

"I'm just making sure the stranger who changed your tire didn't kidnap you."

"Whatever."

"So tell me about this *kind stranger.*"

She blushed at the thought of him, and then giggled like a high school girl. "His name is Steven and that's all I know. Oh, and he looks simply amazing in a suit."

"Did you get a last name? I can do a background check."

"No, I didn't, we didn't exchange information. But I'm fine with that."

"Well…you seemed as if you were beaming so I just thought you may go out with him."

"Syd, for the last time, I'm happy being single.

My main concern is expanding my business. I'm focusing on my career right now."

Megan turned her car into the valet parking area and grabbed her purse from the backseat as the valet guy opened the door, greeted her and handed her a ticket. "I'm here, Syd. I'll see you in a few minutes."

Thirty minutes later, Megan sat at her reserved table after she gave her donation and chatted briefly with her client and mentor, Chelsea Benton, who had invited her to the gala. Megan loved to dress up and hang with her girlfriends in intimate or casual settings but big bashes weren't exactly her cup of tea. However, it was for charity, plus Chelsea had promised to introduce her to some potential clients.

She glanced over at her twin sitting beside her, who seemed to be having a great time people watching.

"Let me guess. You're watching everyone and figuring out what they're thinking just by their body language."

Sydney nodded. Her bob hair cut swished forward in the process. Their hairstyles were the only way people knew who was who. Plus their personalities were like night and day. Megan was the more whimsical, bubbly twin whereas Sydney was the serious-minded and logical one.

"Yes, but not on purpose. It's just a habit. Like right now I can tell by your pursed lips and the way your hand is resting under your chin, that you're ready to leave."

"I am, but I'll stay for a little longer. Chelsea wanted Jade and I to meet some potential clients."

"And where is your best friend?" Sydney glanced around the room.

"Right here, Tia and Tamera," a sassy voice behind them said. "Thank you for saving me a seat."

Jade Whitmore was Megan's best friend from college. Together they owned Chase and Whitmore Designs, an up-and-coming boutique decorating firm for the past six years.

Jade slid into the empty seat on the other side of Megan and placed a glass of champagne on the table. "Sorry I'm late. I had to meet with the Cannadys to pick up their last payment. Glad we're done with that project."

"Me, too," Megan agreed but her attention was diverted by the commotion at the entrance of the event. The ladies and other guests all placed their eyes on a man flanked with bodyguards and an entourage of people strolling into the gala. The man in the middle turned his back to the crowd as he stopped to shake hands and chat with a few people who approached him.

"Must be someone important," Megan shrugged and sipped her champagne as she stared at the back of the tall man clad in a black tuxedo. He turned to the side to greet a lady with a too-short dress on who in return gazed up at him as if he were the most handsome man in the world.

Megan cocked her head to the side and raised an eyebrow as a smile inched across her face and her heart and stomach began to flutter uncontrollably.

"Oh, my goodness!"

Sydney and Jade placed their attention on her, and Sydney waved her hand in front of her twin's face. "I've never seen you smile like that before. I know he's gorgeous, but stop drooling."

Megan shook her head as she tried to calm her smile and excitement down, but it was no use especially when he turned his head as if he sensed her staring at him. Their eyes locked, and a charming smile crept across his breathtaking, chiseled face. He nodded knowingly as he took a step in her direction but a couple stepped in his path for conversation. Even though he conversed with them, his eyes on hers never faltered.

Jade tapped her on the shoulder. "Megan, do you know who you're making goo-goo eyes with?"

She nodded. "Yes, that's him. The man who changed my flat tire."

"That's who changed your tire?" Sydney questioned in a surprised tone.

"Yes and apparently he *is* someone important since everyone seems to know who he is except me."

"Um…yes…" Jade started. "That's Georgia state senator Steven Monroe, self-proclaimed lifelong bachelor and one of Atlanta's most notorious playboys."

Chapter 2

"I'll call you next week about that," Steven promised, shaking his associate's hand as he tried to move away from the crowd of people that were beginning to form around him. His eyes couldn't tear away from Megan's lovely face. He was quite surprised to see her when he entered the ballroom for just some moments ago he'd taken a cold shower as he thought of her. Of course he told himself the cold shower was to cool down his temperature after changing her tire in the blazing evening sun, but he knew that was a lie.

He hadn't been in the mood to attend the fundraiser, but considering it was in the same building he lived in, all he had to do was ride the elevator down to the first floor. Plus, his best friend and campaign manager, Shawn Bennett suggested Steven at least should show his face, shake hands and give a considerable donation. But most importantly stay away from the ladies. His reputation couldn't handle any more bad press considering he had been on local blogs and news channels with a different woman nearly every week. And considering Steven's father wanted him to eventually run for the U.S. Senate seat he was retiring from at the end of the year, Steven needed to first clean up his image. While he would be a shoo-in to win the nomination because of his intellect, clean political slate and charismatic nature, the Monroe campaign team was more concerned that Steven's playboy image would cost him the opportunity to win.

So he'd made a promise to stay low-key and out of the limelight with the ladies and therefore opted not to have a date that evening. However, there was something about Megan that was drawing him to her like a magnetic force. When he entered the room earlier, he sensed the same calming peace he had when he'd initially met her. Was it her perfume in the atmosphere or her cute giggle that made him turn her way, only to find her inquisitive eyes on him? She bestowed her beautiful smile as she had when he'd changed her tire, but this one was accompanied with a look of promise that he couldn't explain. He had a feeling his smile matched hers.

Steven continued to nod and shake hands with people who approached him all the while keeping his eyes glued to Megan and her table. He briefly glanced on either side of her to make sure she didn't have a date. On her left was a woman who looked just like her, which must've been the twin sister she'd mentioned. And the other lady at the table, while drop-dead gorgeous, did nothing for him, either. There weren't any men in their presence, and he was grateful. "Hello, Megan," he said casually. "And ladies." He nodded at them but kept his eyes on Megan. "Nice to see you here. I was hoping to run into someone I know."

She chuckled with a head tilt. "Weren't you just bombarded with people *you know?* We just met an hour ago."

"Hmm…I know, yet we keep running into each other. Maybe we're supposed to be in each other's lives."

She released her signature cute giggle again, and he was glad when her friends excused themselves but not before the both of them winked at Megan. He sat in the chair across from her and dismissed his bodyguards who were actually his campaign manager and his brother, Bryce. They'd tagged along to make sure he stayed out of trouble. And he sensed their hesitancy before they strode away.

"I must say, I'm quite glad to see you. You drove away without me getting any of your information. I don't even know your last name."

"It's Chase. Megan Chase…Senator Monroe," she stated knowingly with a grin.

He threw his head back in laughter. "Does that bother you?"

"Nope. I'm forever grateful. Could you imagine me changing a tire in heels and in this dress?"

His eyes traveled over her body settling on her shapely legs and a glimpse of the side of her exquisite thighs peeking out from her dress.

No, but I can imagine you only in those heels with your legs over my shoulders. He blinked his eyes a few times and cleared the frog in his throat. At first he thought he'd spoken his private thoughts out loud.

"So that means I have your vote in the next election?"

"I don't know," she said in a teasing manner. "What makes you the perfect candidate?"

"I'm a regular down-to-earth guy who likes to help people less fortunate than myself and ultimately make a difference in my community."

"I'm sold. When does your current term end?"

"I just started my second term as a senator for Georgia so not for another two years. However, I'm considering running for a U.S. Senate seat within the next year or so, but let's keep that between us for now. It's my father's seat, and I'm sure there're a few people who would love to have it if they caught wind of my dad retiring."

"Your secret is safe with me," she said sincerely.

Steven couldn't believe he'd told her such secret information so easily. Only he, his father, brother and best friend were aware of Senator Robert Monroe's retirement plans. But for some reason he trusted the lady sitting in front of him.

"So how long have you been in the interior-design business?"

"Well unofficially since I was seven years old." She paused to laugh. "I redesigned my side of my childhood room by using watercolors and markers on the wall. I also cut up some old drapes my mother was going to toss to make throw pillows and a duvet cover. I loved it but much to my mother's dismay, she wasn't pleased with the mural on the wall. But officially when I graduated with my undergraduate degree, so six years."

"I currently live in a penthouse here at Twelve, but it was already furnished. However, I'm looking into buying a home soon and would love to hire a professional decorator."

"I'm always looking for new clients, which is one of the reasons why I'm here. Just let me know when you're ready."

She opened her evening bag and handed him a business card.

He knew it would be months before he would close on a home. He wasn't even officially looking for a house yet although he had an agent. It was just something he was considering, but he couldn't let months go by without seeing her.

"Well, do you have any appointments available this Monday? I would love to see your portfolio and talk to you about some of my ideas."

She nodded and pulled her cell phone out of her purse. "I have Monday around noon available. Is that a good time for you? If not… Friday."

He actually had an appointment on Monday at the exact same time, but he couldn't possibly wait until Friday. He didn't know if he could wait the two days until Monday. "Noon will be fine. How about we meet at a restaurant and have a business lunch?"

"That sounds good. My office is located in the Buckhead area. How about Café Love Jones? It's a jazz club, but they're open for lunch, as well. I have business meetings there quite often."

"That's a great spot. Delicious food and atmosphere."

"Glad you think so. My big brother Braxton is the owner."

"Cool. I don't know him personally, but I met him briefly at an event there a few years ago. Brother can play the hell out of a piano."

Steven then unconsciously glanced up to see Shawn tapping his watch which meant it was time to move on. He was supposed to stay focused, mixing and mingling with the crowd, not flirting with the most beautiful woman at the fund-raiser. But he remembered his promise, and reluctantly stood as the smile on Megan's soft face sank a little.

"It was nice seeing you again, Megan. I look forward to our meeting on Monday."

"Me, too." She held out her hand to shake his, but instead he raised it to his lips and kissed it tenderly. The feel of her silky, warm skin on his lips and the scent of her perfume on her wrist shook him to the core. He let his mouth linger on her hand longer than he should have, as he stared into her cinnamon eyes.

She let out a soft sigh and slowly withdrew her hand from his. He regained his composure and tried to remember where he was before he did something impulsive like pull her into his arms and kiss her until her knees buckled.

Steven cleared his throat and shoved his hands in his pockets to restrain them. "I'll see you later."

For the rest of the evening he socialized with the other guests, discussing politics all while keeping his eyes on Megan. Every now and then he'd catch her glance in his direction as Chelsea Benton escorted her and her friend around. He assumed Chelsea was introducing the women to possible clients since they were eagerly handing out business cards.

An hour later he felt a tap on his shoulder and was pleasantly surprised to look down into Megan's adorable face.

"Hey, pretty lady." He leaned over and whispered in her ear. "Having fun? I saw quite a few gentlemen trying to get to know you better."

"Um…yes, but I'm not trying to date at the present moment. However, I met some potential clients. I just wanted to say thank you again for changing my tire, and I look forward to our meeting on Monday."

"Me, too. Why are you cutting out so early?"

"I'm not really one for social events even though I should be. However, Chelsea insisted that I come."

"How do you know Chelsea Benton?"

"She's one of my mother's best friends from college. And you?"

"Her husband is golf buddies with my father, and

she did some fashion consulting for me both times I ran for the state senate."

"She's the best." Megan then let out a yawn, which caused him to yawn, as well. They both laughed, and he stepped closer toward her.

"Good night, Ms. Chase." His voice was low. Serious. He hoped the stir in his manhood stayed at bay. He wasn't in the mood for any more cold showers that evening.

If she was any other woman, he would've invited her upstairs to his place, but he knew Megan wasn't the type to say yes to that and he was glad she wasn't. Out of all the young women at the fundraiser aside from her twin and girlfriend, Megan was the only one that hadn't either batted her eyelashes and twirled her hair or slipped her phone number in the front of his pants' pocket.

"Good night, Senator Monroe."

He hesitated to leave, but just then her sister arrived to let her know the valet had pulled their cars around, and the two ladies walked away.

"Who was that?" he heard Shawn say as he approached from the side as they both stood in place staring after Megan and her sister.

"The one woman who could possibly make me settle down."

The next morning Megan awoke to the sounds of birds chirping outside the window ledge of her loft apartment and a splitting headache. Usually the echoes of birds soothed her nerves, but not this morning. She wasn't able to sleep last night. Every time she closed her eyes, she fantasized about the handsome Steven Monroe and his strong hands roaming over her figure. Or his lips moving from her hand and wandering over every inch of her body until she passed out from pure ecstasy. She'd almost swooned last night when the caress of his warm lips pressed against her skin sent her to a point of oblivion while she tried to remain composed on the outside. No man had ever stirred her like that before. But she knew getting involved with a politician was out of the question. Or any man for that matter. Right now her focus was her career and a serious relationship was out of the question.

After tossing and turning, Megan had gotten up in the middle of the night and spent a few hours online researching Steven. She'd heard of him before but because she wasn't all that interested in politics, she never paid him much attention, and she didn't read the gossip blogs. She discovered he was divorced but with no children. No mention of a dog, but it was a possibility. Men like him usually had a dog for companionship.

As Megan continued her research, she learned that Steven was a politician that believed that his constituents should be able to voice their opinions. He based his platforms on their concerns as well as his own moral and personal beliefs. As a state senator, he held monthly meetings with the citizens of his district to discuss their needs in the community. Steven had opened a children's after-school center, organized community gardens and raised funds for new roads in poverty stricken areas as well as more funding for the schools in his district. He wasn't afraid to speak his mind, which made him well liked by his constituents though frowned upon by some of his fellow politicians.

The only negative news Megan discovered was that he was dating several different women at the same time. The media labeled him as both an eligible bachelor and playboy. She found that hard to believe considering he was a perfect gentleman the night before and paid no attention to other gorgeous women who threw sexy smiles his way and dirty looks at her. However, there were plenty of pictures of him and beautiful women on the gossip blogs so apparently it was true.

Megan rose from her bed to put on a pot of coffee. Percy, her Persian cat, was staring at her from his heated cat bed on the floor. She was surprised that he wasn't in the bed with her, but sometimes Percy needed his own space. *Just like a male.* She laughed.

Megan sipped on hazelnut-flavored coffee seated at her kitchen's island and reviewed paint colors for her latest project for Chelsea. Chelsea was her role model and mentor. It was because of her that Megan had a steady flow of clients lately. She was supposed to meet Chelsea to look at fabrics in the next hour. Luckily, the store was only within ten minutes of both her loft and office. She decided since it was a lovely April day, she would walk and clear her brain.

After her shower, she threw on some jeans with

a fuchsia T-shirt and pulled her hair into a bouncy ponytail. She glanced at the clock and realized she was ahead of schedule. Grabbing her cell phone, she was surprised to see over twenty missed phone calls and text messages from her cousin Tiffani Chase, Sydney and Jade all within a span of ten minutes. The phone then rang while it was still in her hand. It was Sydney.

"What's up Syd?"

"Wow, don't you sound calm."

"Why wouldn't I be?"

"I guess you haven't seen today's paper or the local gossip blogs this morning."

"I just got up. Haven't been online yet."

"Turn on your computer and go to the Atlanta Social website.

Megan went into her living room where her tablet sat on the coffee table. She opened the website Syd mentioned and almost dropped her tablet on the hardwood floor. On the screen were pictures from the fund-raiser last night, but the main picture of the article was of her and Steven when he kissed her hand. The accompanying caption read, "Who's the senator's new lady of the week?"

"Oh, no." Megan sighed and sank onto the couch. "This can't be happening." She scrolled through some more of the event pictures, and there were four more of them laughing and having a good time.

"Girl, those aren't the only pictures of you two. I'm at the GBI office and one of the agents just brought me the social section of the newspaper.

There's another one where Steven is leaning over whispering in your ear, and you're staring at him like a lovesick puppy with your eyes half closed."

"We were just talking. I'm not dating the senator. Why would they print this?"

"Calm down, sis. This happens to him all the time. You just don't keep up. It'll all blow over I'm sure. He'll be on the same blog tomorrow with a different woman, and no one will give you a second thought."

"But this has never happened to *me* before. I don't want my reputation ruined with my clients because they think I'm dating a playboy politician. No, wait. It says 'lady of the week.' That's even worse." Megan looked at a few more local blogs she found through Google, and the same pictures with similar captions popped up.

"Try not to worry about it," Sydney said in a sincere tone. "They don't even know your name."

Megan's phone beeped with another phone call. *Perfect.*

"Our mother is calling me on the other line."

"Now you can worry. Don't answer."

"I'm not. I can only imagine what she's going to say."

"Chin up, sis. I have a meeting, but call me if you need to."

After hanging up, the phone rang again but this time from a number she didn't recognize. She decided to answer it anyway just in case it was a potential client.

"Hello?" she answered cautiously.

"Hey, Megan this is Steven."

"Oh, joy. It's the playboy politician," she said sarcastically as she walked to her bedroom that was separated from the living room with a sliding wall. She grabbed her purse and keys from the bench in front of the bed. She needed to head out soon to meet Chelsea.

"I guess you saw the blogs this morning."

"Yes, I did, and I'm not amused at all. I don't even know you! We just met yesterday."

"I'm so sorry this has happened. Trust me last night I was supposed to mix and mingle and not flirt. I'm trying to clean up my image if I'm going to run for my dad's seat, but whenever the media sees me with a woman they assume I'm seeing her...which sometimes I am."

"Maybe if you stop kissing women's hands and whispering in their ears, your photo won't get taken as much," she snapped.

He chuckled, and her breath caught in her throat. She was supposed to be mad, but how could she when his seductive voice was in her ear reminding her of the tossing and turning she did last night over him?

"You have a point, but my team sent a statement to all of the blogs and news outlets that have the pictures that we aren't dating, and that you're an interior decorator who will be working on some projects for me in the future, all of which is true."

She let out a sigh of relief. She knew it wasn't his

fault that this had happened. He was a politician from a very prestigious family so naturally he would be in the limelight. Too bad his playboy past was getting him in trouble even when the situation was innocent. While she had just met him, he seemed like a cool, down-to-earth guy. Maybe the media blew his reputation out of proportion.

"Thank you for releasing the statement. I know it's not your fault, but it did shake me up because I live a simple, drama-free life. And I like to keep it that way."

"I completely understand. I wish my life was simple at times. So, are we still on for this Monday?"

"Yes, of course. Remember, I'm not really the lady of the week, I'm the interior decorator you'll be working with." She laughed.

"I'll keep that in mind. Besides, you aren't 'lady of the week' material. More like the lady forever, and I would hate for anyone to think otherwise."

The heat in her cheeks began to rise, and she had a feeling they would be burning red if she looked in a mirror.

"Thank you. I hate to cut this conversation short, but I have a meeting in a few minutes."

"On a Saturday?"

"Normally I wouldn't schedule a meeting on a Saturday, but it's Chelsea."

"Cool. Give her my best."

After saying their goodbyes, Megan grabbed her tablet and purse and headed out the door. She felt somewhat better since Steven called.

While browsing through material in the fabric store, Sydney sent her a text that a statement had been released about her and Steven's platonic relationship and the blogs had been updated. She decided she wasn't going to worry about it. Like her sister said, it would all blow over, and some other woman would be in a picture with him tomorrow. The thought of that made her a little sad, but she knew he was the last man she should be involved with even if the very thought of him caused her to go weak.

Her main focus was expanding her business and taking it to the next level. Her and Jade were in the process of landing a guest spot on the famed show *Decorator's Dream* on the Fabulous Living Channel. They'd sent in pictures of all of their decorating jobs over the past few years and their audition video. Now they were on pins and needles waiting to hear back. Plus, much to her family and friends' dismay, Megan actually enjoyed being single at this time in her life. She shook her head to wipe the thought of dating Steven out of her mind. From now on, she would think of him as a potential client. Nothing more.

Chapter 3

"Steven, we have one more topic to discuss," Shawn Bennett said uneasily to his best friend.

Steven sat at the desk in his downtown office while Bryce and Shawn sat in the leather wingback chairs in front. They'd been discussing the latest comments about Steven from the media including gossip blogs and social media. He had begun to tune them out after a while considering it was the same conversation that'd been had over and over.

Instead, his thoughts began to wander to Megan. He couldn't seem to get her bubbly personality, cute smile, flirty eyes or whimsical voice out of his head. He didn't know which was cuter: the way she spoke or the sparkle in her eyes when she laughed. He was eager to leave for their lunch meeting just to resolve which one.

He glanced at the clock on the opposite wall and then back at the two men in front of him that he'd momentarily forgot were there. *Maybe if I pay attention to them we could speed this boring meeting up.*

"What else do we need to talk about?" he asked nonchalantly.

Bryce cleared his throat, stood up from his seat and positioned himself in front of his brother.

"Ok, big brother. It's like this. We feel that you have a wonderful platform and a good chance of winning the nomination for Dad's seat. There are constituents who will vote for you because of who you are plus they agree with your views on certain issues. You're a great senator. But because of the way you've been portrayed in the media, people may not take you seriously as a U.S. senator," Bryce said as he paced back and forth around the room. "Your escapades have caught national attention lately since there's a buzz going around about Dad retiring at the end of his term."

"Man, maybe you need to slow down some with the ladies," Shawn added. "You know…save some of the action for me and Bryce."

Steven looked at his brother and his best friend. He'd been friends with Shawn since their days at Harvard, and he always had his back. Steven knew they were both right. He wasn't trying to have a reputation as a playboy, he just happened to enjoy the company of different women. Some spent the night and some didn't. And after the last incident at the ski resort in Colorado with an alleged threesome, the media was following his every move.

"Steven, is there someone in your life you can date exclusively?" Bryce asked.

"No, not really. They were mostly one-nighters. And I don't mean one night stands, necessarily. Just one date and then I wasn't interested anymore." Steven thought over the list of women he'd been out with or slept with lately. Even though only one woman was occupying his mind at the moment.

"What about the interior decorator you were photographed with?" Shawn offered. "You two were having a grand time at the fund-raiser event. The shutterbugs couldn't get enough."

"We have a meeting at noon to discuss her possibly decorating my house... Once I find one and buy it, of course. But I doubt she would want to go out with me. She's already called me the playboy politician."

"This is exactly our point. You can easily lose the female vote if women only see you as a playboy," Bryce said.

Steven thought about what Bryce said for a moment and then gave a cocky smile.

"Or the opposite. You know, some women will vote for me because they think I'm a good-looking playboy. Have you seen these dimples? Women go crazy!" Steven said trying not to brag and more so lighten the mood of the room.

"Oh, you find this funny?" Bryce asked in an irritated tone. "The Monroe name is on the line. Our family has worked hard for generations in order to become established and to be taken seriously in the political world. Dad has groomed us for this, and you're not going to ruin my chances of becoming a district attorney one day. Plus, Jacqueline is considering going into politics, so don't ruin this for our baby sister. Shape up and get it together."

Steven nodded as he listened to his brother. He knew he was right. Fun and games were over. He was a grown man. He was a Monroe man. He knew his family was influential in politics thanks to his grandfather and father.

"What do you need me to do?"

"Cut out this playboy persona and settle down with one woman to improve your chances to win the nomination. You need to be seen in the media as a good guy and a devoted boyfriend. Ever since your divorce, you've been on this wild roller-coaster ride for the last ten years. It's time to get off."

His divorce. It should have been an annulment, but his ex-wife, Veronica, wanted the prenuptial agreement to stand so she could receive her settlement should they ever part. After only six months of marriage, Steven knew it was hopeless. Veronica had only married him because he was a Monroe. When he realized that she never loved him, he was crushed. He thought she was the one when he saw her studying in the library while both law students at Harvard. Apparently she'd done her homework and was determined to be his wife. Over the years, they remained cordial running into each at events or speaking engagements. She was now a law professor at a college in Washington, D.C., thanks to his last name that she refused to drop no matter how many millions she was offered during the divorce settlement.

Since they'd parted ways, he dated, but nothing serious ever came out of it. And once he realized they were only interested in the Monroe name, he dropped them, thus igniting his persona in the media.

"I hear you, Bryce. Which one of my past conquests should I consider?"

"Actually, Megan Chase would be the perfect candidate. You've already been photographed with her, and you two appeared quite cozy."

"Yes," Shawn said as he grabbed a folder from his briefcase. "We did a little research as always when you're photographed with a new woman. She's twenty-seven years old. According to her DMV records, she's five feet six inches and weighs 125 pounds. Her father is a principal at a local high school and her mother is a first grade teacher. They were high school sweethearts and have been married for thirty-five years. Ms. Chase has never had any arrests, and has only had one speeding ticket. She won a full scholarship to Clark Atlanta University and started her interior-decorating business out of her parent's basement along with her best friend when they graduated from college. But now they have an office in Buckhead.

"Ms. Chase's twin sister is a GBI agent and their older brother is a musician who owns a jazz club/

restaurant here in Atlanta. Her uncle on her mother's side is Dr. Francis Arrington, a world renowned heart surgeon in Memphis and all his children are doctors, as well. She likes hanging with her family and her girlfriends. Her ex-boyfriend is a doctor here in Atlanta. She helped him start his practice, but they broke up about a year and a half ago once she found out he was cheating with one of his nurses."

"Wow. Do you know her blood type, too?" Steven asked sarcastically. Shawn had done research before but never to this extent.

Shawn glanced through some papers in his folders. "Yes. She's AB."

Steven chuckled. "I was just joking."

"We aren't," Bryce stated in a firm tone. "This is serious."

"Anything else I need to know about Ms. Chase? Is she lactose intolerant? How does she like her eggs prepared?"

"Yes. She's trying to get a spot on the show *Decorator's Dream*." Shawn closed the folder and laid it on Steven's desk.

Steven then glanced down at it and shook his head in disbelief. "Well, I'm not sure if I'm totally on board with this absurd idea, but I'll give it some thought."

Megan sat nervously in the parking lot of her brother's restaurant on Peachtree Street downtown. She'd called Braxton ahead of time to tell him she was coming because she wanted to make sure her favorite booth was available because it overlooked the stage. It was the perfect spot for when jazz bands played in the evenings and occasionally during lunch.

She tapped her steering wheel nervously, trying to decide whether or not she should restart her SUV and drive home before Steven showed up. She knew it was just a business luncheon, but for some reason she felt as if they were going on a first date. Taking a deep breath, she checked her hair and makeup in the visor mirror before stepping out of the car and walking toward the front door of the restaurant. She saw her reflection in the glass doors and stopped briefly to make sure she looked presentable. She had decided to wear a pair of dress jeans with a white tee, a pink seersucker blazer and wedged sandals. Her hair was curly and swooped to one side over her shoulder. Huge gold hoop earrings and a charm bracelet completed the casual look.

She tried to tell herself that this meeting wasn't a big deal but deep down she was nervous. He made her nervous. Not because he was a politician or a millionaire. She'd dealt with people of his social status before. She was nervous because she knew somewhere inside of her, she wanted him and that scared her. She'd been on quite a few dates thanks to her girls playing matchmaker but none of the men had flustered her to this point. None of them had kept her up at night with sinful thoughts that made her cheeks turn pink like Steven had. His scent. His smile. The seductive way he gazed at her when he kissed her hand, were all imbedded in her brain.

"Megan!"

She looked up to see Steven walking down the elegant staircase of the restaurant. He, too, had dressed casually in khaki dress pants and a red golf shirt. His smile was simply charming, and she couldn't help but return it as she walked toward him. She began to get a little wobbly in the knees, and she couldn't stop smiling at the magnificent man in front of her. *Heaven help me!*

When Steven saw Megan looking up at him from the bottom of the staircase, he was captivated. He thought the dress she'd worn when he met her was sexy, but there she stood in jeans even sexier, and she wasn't even trying.

"Wow, you look great," he said, reaching out his hand to her to lead her back upstairs. "Our table is up here. I was told it's your favorite."

Once seated, the waiter took their drink and lunch order. Thirty minutes later, they were eating shrimp po' boys and fries and laughing at all of the blind dates Megan had been on lately.

"So let me get this straight," Steven said, amused, "This dude was on a date with you trying to sell you a time-share?" He laughed again, taking a sip of his tea. "Did you buy one?"

"No, I declined. Then he tried to tell me about some other get-rich-quick scheme. I have tons of stories."

"Why do your family and friends keep setting you up? You're breathtaking. I would assume men ask you out all of the time."

She lowered her head and tried to stifle a smile when he mentioned she was breathtaking. He didn't want to embarrass her. He was merely speaking the truth. She twirled a French fry around in the ketchup before looking back up and answering him.

"They do, but I always cancel at the last minute or find some reason not to go on a second date. My girlfriends say I'm just being picky so they set me up with guys that they think would be perfect for me."

"So how many dates are we going to go on before you decide to dump me, too?" he asked jokingly.

"This isn't a date. We're supposed to be discussing decorating your future home. You haven't even looked at my portfolio yet." She reached into her oversize leather tote bag and pulled out her tablet and slid it across the table to him.

"To be honest, I'm having such a great time that I forgot this was supposed to be business luncheon. My meetings are usually with old men discussing politics, investments and golf. Not with an adorable woman cracking me up with her blind-date history."

"Trust me they weren't that funny to be on, that's for sure. I've asked my friends both politely and rudely to stop."

"Why do they keep setting you up? Did something happen in a past relationship?" he asked, thinking about what Shawn read earlier.

"Ever since my last long-term relationship ended, they think I'm lonely for a man because all I do is work. But what they fail to realize is that I'm happy being single. I enjoy my freedom. I was with my ex for almost four years and my world was centered on him. I helped him start his medical practice right after I started my interior-decorating business with Jade. I began to lose sight of my dreams and ambitions that he wasn't even being supportive of in the first place. After I found out he was cheating with a nurse in his office, I dumped him and focused on me and building my business. I'm not lonely, but no one seems to understand except me."

"They sound like my brother and campaign manager. Just earlier today, they were telling me to settle down with one person. They think that would somehow improve my image and give me a better shot of winning the nomination for my father's seat."

"Well, you are a self-proclaimed playboy," she said, shrugging her shoulders and rolling her eyes away from his with a grin.

He chuckled at her sarcasm. "The media says that. Truth is, I've been married before—didn't work out. Like you, I enjoy my single life. No strings. No attachments. No hearts to break."

"I wish I could just tell my family and friends I have a boyfriend so they can stop harassing me." She threw the cloth napkin from her lap into her plate and sat back in her seat.

Steven studied her angelic face, which at the moment appeared disturbed. He knew what she was going through. But now that he'd had met Megan, he wanted to get to know her better. Even though, it seemed as if she wanted to be single and free. Heck, so did he, but he knew he needed to settle down his dating habits and clean up his image if he wanted to win the nomination. Most of the potential candidates for his father's seat were either engaged or married with families, summer homes and of course a beloved dog. He didn't even have a dog.

As he watched Megan, he saw the epitome of what he wanted in a woman. Graceful, refined, sexy without having to try, successful and independent. He was ready to learn about her other qualities, as well.

"You know Megan, you could just tell them you're dating me."

"But that would be a lie," she answered, shaking her head.

"It wouldn't have to be."

"Steven, that's ridiculous. We can't do that."

"Think about it. Your family and friends want you to date and be happy. My campaign team feels I need to stick with one person. Why not?"

"Because it wouldn't be right. It would be dishonest, and I know despite your escapades with women, you're an honest politician. You're a good man, Steven."

"Thank you, but I need someone like you and…" he paused as he thought about something else Shawn said earlier. "You need me."

She leaned over the table toward him and whispered, "I don't need to date you in name only to please my family and friends. Besides, I have a blossoming career thanks in part to having more free time to concentrate on it instead of cater to an ungrateful man."

"Really?"

"Yes, really." She sat back against her booth seat.

He leaned forward and whispered, "I can get you more clients and a chance to meet with the bigwigs of the Fabulous Living Channel. You can showcase your work on an upcoming show they're doing this summer."

She blinked her lashes several times and stared in disbelief. *"Decorator's Dream?"* she asked, leaning in toward him again with her eyes wide. Steven grabbed her hands in his when he thought he heard her heart beating faster.

"Yep, that show."

"How do you know about that show? They're only in the early-production stages."

"I know the creator."

"Justine Monroe? Jade and I sent her a copy of our portfolio and the audition video three months ago…" She stopped. She seemed to be pondering something, and Steven hoped it was a yes to his question. "Monroe…? Is she your ex-wife?"

"No. First cousin. I could put in a good word for you if…"

"If I agree to date you…in name only."

"Why do you keeping saying in name only? Am I not to get any *special* benefits?"

"You'll have the benefit of me on your arm, no more."

"So, that's a yes, Ms. Chase?"

"If I decide to do this, are you still going to see other women on the side?" Megan asked seriously.

"No, I don't intend to date anyone else. Unlike what you've read or heard through the grapevine about me, I don't have dozens of girlfriends."

"I'm sure the word *girlfriend* isn't in your vocabulary. So why me?"

"Because I need a successful, intelligent and classy woman such as yourself on my arm," he said. "Plus, you're the quintessential girl-next-door, which is the type of woman I need in order to clean up my image."

"Don't you have plenty of other female friends to ask? I read the gossip sites. There are tons of pictures with you and drop-dead gorgeous women. Supermodels, actresses, singers…someone more on your level."

"I don't want a woman like that. They get boring. They only care about fame, material things and spending my money. I want someone I can talk to. Someone to stimulate my mind. Someone to laugh with like you've made me do for the past hour. And I can save you from more horrible dates. So, yes I'd say you're the perfect candidate."

"Perfect candidate? I'm not the one running for office."

"But will you be by my side when I do?"

Chapter 4

The next morning Megan woke up earlier than normal. She wasn't a morning person, but she could no longer sleep after tossing and turning with Steven's request on her mind. He told her to think about it, and if they chose to go forward with their plans, they agreed to tell no one.

She decided to jog on her treadmill and listen to some music. She was nervous about what the future held. But at least she wouldn't have to worry about any blind dates for a while because she would be in an exclusive relationship with Senator Steven Monroe.

Her main fear was that he'd sleep with women on the side, but it wouldn't be cheating because they weren't in a real relationship. Though, he had said he wouldn't, and she believed him. Megan wondered how her ex would feel about her dating a senator. He probably wouldn't care. He definitely didn't care about her feelings when he lied and cheated on her for almost four years.

She was going to get on with her life and if that meant helping a senator clean up his image, then that's was what she was going to do. Plus, if it meant having a shot to land a guest spot on *Decorator's Dream* then it was well worth it. Satisfied with her decision, she jumped off of the treadmill, showered, dressed and headed out the door to Chase and Whitmore Designs.

When Megan arrived, Jade was speaking to the intern, Lucy, in the mostly all-white reception area that Lucy had recently remodeled for a class project. Megan, who loved antiques, was quite impressed with Lucy's mixture of modern and Louis XVI–style furniture. Light blue and lavender toss pillows laden the white chairs and couches in the client waiting area. Fresh calla lilies and orchids sat on end tables along with decorating books.

Megan smiled as she looked at her best friend. She was truly the diva of fashion and style. Her makeup was flawless which added to her large brown eyes and her auburn-colored skin. Her shoulder-length layered dark hair was curled without a strand out of place. She wore an off-white pantsuit with stilettos making her even taller than her already five-foot-seven-inch height.

"Are you forgetting our job today?" Megan inquired looking down at her khaki capris, tennis shoes and a sleeveless pink T-shirt. Her long hair was pulled back into a bun at her neck. "We're hanging wallpaper."

"I have a change of clothes in the car. Besides, that appointment isn't until this afternoon, and I have another appointment in an hour with Wade Greene, you know the sportscaster." Jade looked up from the file she was reading. "Chelsea introduced me to him at her cocktail party last month. After seeing what we did with her home, he now wants me to redo his dining and living room areas. Still, I promise to be at the Brown's to help you hang wallpaper. I just need to show him some fabric swatches for his dining room."

"And get a date?" Megan questioned her single friend.

"If I'm lucky." Jade winked and then sashayed back to her office.

"I'm going to run down to Starbucks for a caramel macchiato," Megan said, heading toward the door.

"I can go get it for you, Ms. Chase," Lucy offered. She was an eager-to-please intern. Lucy had one more semester before graduation, and Megan was contemplating hiring her full-time.

"No, I need to run a quick errand, as well. I'll be back in a few." She really didn't have to go to Starbucks considering they had a Keurig in the kitchen, but she wanted to go ahead and call Steven with her answer before she changed her mind. And she didn't want to do it in her office. She rarely closed her door when she was there because Jade and Lucy were always in and out. She didn't want them to think something was wrong, and she definitely didn't want anyone to else to know about her arrangement with Steven.

When she walked into the Starbucks, she found an empty table near the back. She figured she would order enough coffee and pastries for everyone before she left. She then nervously dialed Steven's cell phone number. She couldn't believe what she was about to do.

At exactly seven that evening, Megan's phone rang. She was sitting on the floor brushing Percy, a weekly ritual that he hated. She glanced at the caller ID and saw Steven's name. He was in a meeting earlier when she called him with her decision. They agreed to talk that evening, and he was punctually calling at the time she'd suggested.

She stood up to grab her notepad that she had earlier jotted some general questions in to ask Steven. Free from Megan's hands, Percy darted out of the bedroom to escape the brushing ritual.

"Hello?" Megan plopped down on the bed.

"Hey, it's Steven. How are you doing this evening?"

"Fine, Stevo. And how are you?"

"Stevo?" he asked taken aback.

"Well, I figured you need a pet name for me to call you. You don't like Stevo?"

"No, it reminds me of my days in high school when the nerds would call me Stevo or worse Stevster."

"I see. Well, I guess we'll think of something else. In the meantime, I have some questions that every girlfriend should know," Megan said getting her pen ready.

"Yes, I have big feet and great hands to give body massages with," he joked.

Megan felt her face getting hot at the thought of his great hands giving her a body massage with hot oil. A man with big feet could only mean one thing, at least most of the time. She smiled at the thought.

"I already have my list of questions."

"That's fine. How was your day?"

"It was good, and yours?"

"I spent most of the day reviewing a possible campaign budget with Shawn just in case I receive the nomination. I need to do some fund-raising if I'm to have a successful campaign."

"I thought all you needed was a great platform and a speech," Megan said, sounding a little naive on that subject. She was never one for keeping up with politics.

He chuckled softly before answering her.

"That's part of it, but I also have to rent the head-quarters, pay people to work there or find volunteers, buy materials, pay for advertisements, but that's not my biggest dilemma at the moment. The community center that I started and help fund is losing one of its grants, therefore losing about ten college students that would normally assist with events with the children during the summer camp."

"Can you do a fund-raiser?"

"Yes, I'm considering hosting a fund-raiser party and then writing a check to match whatever is raised. The grant funded quite a bit."

"Well, maybe I can help." Megan was always one for volunteering her services or expertise if the need arose. "I'm the assistant graduate advisor for one of the undergrad chapters for my sorority. I'll check to see if some of the girls would like to volunteer their services this summer. A lot of them are education majors so they need the experience of working with children," she said, taking notes. The undergrads were having their last meeting of the semester the following evening, and she could approach the ones that were staying in Atlanta for the summer.

"That is very thoughtful and supportive of you."

"No problem. Also, I have a few clients and friends that could possibly give a donation. And I'm sure Braxton won't mind you using the mezzanine level at his restaurant. Let me make some phone calls tomorrow and work my magic, that's if you want me to." She hoped she wasn't overstepping her bounds. Though she was only supposed to play the make-believe girlfriend, planning and organizing were her specialties.

"No, that's wonderful. Thank you," he said in amazement.

"No problem. Isn't that what girlfriends are for?" she asked jokingly.

"Yes, they are. There're some other things girlfriends are good for, as well," Steven said in a sexy tone.

"If you're going to continue talking like that, the

deal is off. Now on to my list of questions," she said getting back to the real business at hand. As much as she liked Steven, Megan knew that sex was one road she couldn't travel with him. For if she did, she'd never want to let him go.

Over the next hour, Megan learned that Steven liked to fish, and listen to jazz, classical, R&B and hip-hop. He played the guitar and gave lessons to the children during the summer camp. He was a running back during his freshman year of college but got hurt and decided not to play anymore. He never wanted to go professional, but he enjoyed football. His parents were relieved he could no longer play, especially his father who wanted him to follow in his footsteps and go into politics. He loved seafood especially shrimp, and he liked Bruce Lee movies. His pet peeve was people who complained about issues but did nothing to make a change. It was also the reason he decided to go into politics and not become a practicing attorney like Bryce. He had a brownstone in Washington, D.C., that he shared with his brother and a townhome in historic Savannah.

"Do you feel that you really know me now?" he asked in a low, deep voice that sent goose bumps down her arms. This man was driving her insane, and she didn't know how much longer she could stand having his voice in her ear.

"Overall." She put down her pen and notepad as Percy jumped into her lap. "I'm sure I'll learn more in the months to come. But I just thought of something else. When I was online looking at pictures of you, I only saw you with a bunch of females. There were only a few family pictures and some of you giving speeches during your last campaign. However, there was nothing with you and the good you do for the communities in your district such as the center and the gardens. Why is that?"

"Well one reason is that all the media and gossip blogs tend to care about is who I'm dating. Plus, I do what I do for my community because it's my passion. I'm not doing it for the publicity. I do it because I care, and I'm in the position to make a change. Everyone wasn't born wealthy like me, but it doesn't mean they can't have the same advantages. There're some articles out there though, about some of the things I've done, but unfortunately my past lifestyle outweighs the good."

"We're going to change that, Steven. It'll help with cleaning up your image. They need to see you playing the guitar with the children and getting dirty in the community garden. They need to see your philanthropy side not the philandering one. I have a reporter friend at one of the local news stations. I'll see if she can come to the fund-raiser."

He laughed. "Wow. Are you an interior decorator or an image consultant?"

"I'm the woman who believes in you and what you stand for."

"Thank you. That truly means a lot to me. Out of all of the women I've dated, including my ex-wife, you've been the only one to say that, and you're not even my real girlfriend. I don't know what I'm going to do without you when this ends. Promise me we'll always be friends."

"Of course." A lump formed in her throat. She didn't want to think about the end. Clearing her windpipe, she glanced at her notepad to see was there anything else she forgot to ask.

"I read somewhere that you don't drink alcohol. Is that true?"

"I may have an occasional glass of wine or champagne, but only when I'm in the comforts of my own home. I wouldn't want the media to snap a picture of me holding a drink. Then I'd be labeled as an alcoholic."

"Makes sense." *I guess he already has enough labels.*

"And you?"

"Occasionally a glass of wine or some girlie drink like Sex on the Beach."

"You like having sex on the beach? Me, too. I own some beachfront property if you ever want to…" Steven said in a teasing manner although she knew he meant it. She tried to ignore his comment even though a picture of them making love on the beach popped into her head.

"Steven, if we're going to do this, you have to refrain from flirting so much." *Because its making me want to jump through the phone and onto your lap.*

"I can't help it. If I can't flirt with you, who am I going to flirt with? You're my girlfriend, but I'll try to keep it to a minimum if it's making you want me."

"Want you? Who says I want you?"

"I know you have to be attracted to me to even do this and that goes both ways. I was going to ask you out anyway. Who knows? Maybe this is a way for us to be a couple and get to know each other in the process. You know, skip the courting part. Besides, you don't like dates."

She laughed sarcastically. "You know, you're funny. If you don't get the nomination, you can always go into comedy. Anyway, a little about me. I was born and raised here in Atlanta. My dad is a high school principal and my mother is a first grade teacher. My hobbies are reading suspense and romance novels, going to the movies and comedy shows. I also listen to most music genres and my favorite singer is Beyoncé. Anything else you care to know?"

She was ready to get off of the phone. She had three meetings all before noon the next day. Plus his low, sexy voice in her ear was starting to wreak havoc on her thought process, and she was beginning to wish he really was her boyfriend. And his sex-on-the-beach comment had made her rather hot in a certain area, and she needed a cold shower. *Fast.* He was quite flirtatious all of sudden, and she didn't know how she was going to make it the next few months if he was constantly flirting with her. He may just receive a special bonus after all.

"What's your favorite flower?" he asked.

"Pink roses and red tulips."

"Why tulips?" he asked curiously.

"My grandfather used to plant them in his garden when I was a little girl. When he died, they bloomed so beautiful that year. But after that they stopped coming back," Megan said getting teary eyed. "Please continue with your questions. I get emotional sometimes thinking about him."

"I completely understand. What's your favorite color?"

"Pink but I also like purple."

"You are such a girlie girl. And favorite perfume?"

"Amarige by Givenchy."

"Is that what you were wearing the day I met you?"

"Yes, it was. That's all I ever wear. Anything else? I really need to get going to type up a budget proposal for a client." She really didn't mean to get that personable with him. She'd never even told her ex the reason why she loved tulips. Perhaps because he'd never asked.

"Yes. That's all for now. Have a good evening, Megan."

"The same to you, Mr. Monroe," she answered hanging up the phone quickly.

A minute later, the phone rang again. *What now?*

"Yes?" Megan answered in an annoyed tone. She was lying on her bed still trying to get the image of sex on the beach out of her head. However, all she kept fantasizing about was lying naked with Steven on a beach towel with those strong hands of his roaming over her body and his lips placing hot kisses on her neck.

"I sometimes wish caller ID hadn't been invented. That way you wouldn't have to answer the phone with such an attitude," Steven said jokingly.

"But answering machines do exist," Megan said impatiently getting up and walking over to her sewing room. She needed to get away from her bed especially with his voice in her ear.

"You still have an answering machine?"

"No."

"I won't keep you on the phone. I just wanted to tell you thank you for helping me. I sincerely appreciate it."

"You are a good man and an honest politician despite your jaunts with women. The only thing I ask of you is that you remain honest with me," Megan said to him seriously.

"That's a promise I can keep. However, by the end of this, you're not going to want to let me go. Good night, Megan."

She sat at her sewing machine and dropped her forehead on it. His words played in her head like a broken record. *What I have I gotten myself into?*

Megan was supposed to be working on a project board for a presentation next week. However, she'd found herself unable to concentrate at home, so she'd headed to the office thinking that her thoughts of Steven wouldn't follow her there. But as she sat in her office staring at a blank board, she was so wrong.

It had been a week since Megan had agreed to be Steven's girlfriend. She hadn't seen him and a part of her was happy about that. However, she found herself missing him and that scared her. Whenever the phone rang, she hoped it was him and in some instances it was. He was out of town on business, but they spoke every day because she was planning a Jazz Wine Down Wednesday fund-raiser for the community center. She was able to reserve space in Braxton's restaurant, which was donating the food and wine. She was also able to invite people from the media. She had secured eight of the undergrads from her sorority, and six undergrads from Steven's fraternity had signed up to volunteer during the summer. Megan had negotiated that the fraternity and sorority members wouldn't be paid, but Steven would write letters of recommendation when they graduated from college, and he would attend a voter's registration drive on campus sponsored by his fraternity.

Megan hadn't told her parents she was dating Steven yet. But she figured they would know by tomorrow morning considering that night's fund-raiser event would be their first outing in public. She did tell Jade, Tiffani and Sydney that she was helping Senator Monroe plan a fund-raiser for the community center. She also casually told them she was his date for the evening. They were excited for her especially since they were invited. Jade only went to A-list events and Tiffani was glad to get out of the house and away from her four-year-old son and his recent tantrums. Ever since Tiffani's husband died of a heart attack almost a year ago, her son had been acting out. Sydney even voluntarily cancelled the date she had set up for Megan to go on the following week, much to her relief.

Megan sat at her desk contemplating her decision to date Steven. While she was indeed attracted to him, the fear of falling for him had weighed heavily on her mind since the day she accepted. Every time she thought about him, her heart thumped hard against her chest and her mind wandered to a place of lust and fantasy with him.

Lucy tapped on the ajar door interrupting Megan's amorous thoughts.

"Ms. Chase, you have a special delivery!" Lucy excitedly announced zooming into the office with her bouncy red hair and blue eyes sparkling brightly. She took Megan by the hand and pulled her out into the reception area. On Lucy's desk, were two dozen pink roses with red tulips scattered throughout in a sparkling crystal vase with a pink-and-lavender chiffon ribbon tied around it.

"Open the card. Open the card." Lucy jumped up and down like a little schoolgirl.

Megan remained speechless. Jade tapped her foot impatiently and placed her hands on her hips giving Megan a "hurry up" look.

"Girl, open the card and stop looking surprised! You know it's from the senator!" Jade demanded handing Megan the card from the bouquet.

Megan really wasn't sure if she wanted to open it in front of them. *Why is he sending me flowers in the first place? This isn't a real relationship!* But she opened the card anyway, if only to appease Lucy and Jade.

"Can't wait to see you tonight. Yours truly, Stevo." She giggled at the way he'd signed his name. *I guess he liked the nickname after all.*

She tried to act overwhelmed in front of Jade and Lucy even though she really didn't have to act at all. She was flattered.

"Oh, these are so beautiful. He remembered my favorite flowers," she said, pleasantly surprised by his gesture.

Now she realized why he asked what her favorite flower was. She was rather pleased that he had sent them and was even more elated of the added extra details of the color of the ribbons. For once, she had found a man that knew what she wanted. *Too bad he's not really my man,* she thought. Too bad her ex never thought like that. She remembered when he sent her yellow roses for her birthday after the fact because he was too busy with patients. She later discovered he was rather getting busy with his nurse at a hotel downtown.

Blushing, Megan took the arrangement to her office and placed it on her desk.

"Ms. Chase," Lucy called after her, "You have a phone call holding on line three. It's Justine Monroe from the Fabulous Living Channel."

Megan ran out of her office and collided with Jade as they immediately locked wide eyes, and then headed straight to the conference room and closed the door.

Jade sat down and stared at the phone. "Girl, this could be it! I'll pray while you answer the phone."

Megan took a deep breath before answering. She pushed the speaker button so Jade could hear, as well.

"This is Megan Chase here also with Jade Whitmore."

"Good morning, ladies. This is Justine Monroe with the Fabulous Living Channel. I have some fabulous news to share with you."

The women locked eyes again, and Jade stood up above the phone and placed her hand over her heart.

"I'm happy to say after reviewing your portfolio as well as the audition video, we would like to offer you and Ms. Whitmore the opportunity to have a segment on *Decorator's Dream.*

"Oh, Ms. Monroe, I... Thank you. We're very excited." Megan sat in the chair in front of the phone and tried to remain composed as she and Jade squeezed hands.

"Craig, my production assistant and I look forward to working with you this summer in Hilton Head. I have to go, but Craig will be in contact with you within the next few days with all of the necessary information you'll need."

"Thank you so much for the opportunity, Ms. Monroe."

After they hung up, the women gave each other huge hugs before running out to the reception area to inform Lucy.

"Now Lucy," Jade, began in a serious tone. "We'll

be gone for a couple of weeks this summer. Think you can hold down the fort while we're away?"

"Yes, Ms. Whitmore. It'll give me a chance to do some projects on my own."

While Jade and Lucy conversed, Megan thought about how quickly Justine called so soon after she spoke to Steven about the opportunity. She made a mental note to call Steven and thank him. She sighed, he had already lived up to his part of the deal, but now she had to do her part. *Why does mine seem so much harder?*

Chapter 5

The evening of the fund-raiser arrived sooner than Megan realized. She left a voice mail on her parent's home phone explaining her plans for that night so they wouldn't be in total shock if there was a picture of her and Steven in newspaper the next day. They had seen the other pictures but once they saw the statement Steven's team had released, her parents had admitted they felt better. She knew they wouldn't be home because of PTA meetings, so a voice mail was perfect. She knew sooner or later they would find out about him so she opted for the later.

Megan stood at her vanity putting the last touches of her makeup on. Steven was sending a car to pick her up, which was to arrive in thirty minutes, and she still hadn't decided on which dress she was going to wear. She'd just gotten out of the shower, but she felt herself perspiring with anxiety. She went into her bedroom and turned on the ceiling fan even though she already had the air conditioner on full blast and tossed the bathrobe on the bed. Percy just stared at her and purred.

"What am I going to wear?" she asked the cat who was now licking his paws. She walked back into the closet and looked at her evening wear and opted for a fuchsia, spaghetti strap dress with a flared, flirty skirt that stopped at her knees showcasing her smooth, freshly waxed legs.

She buckled her heels and then smiled. She was glad that Jade had convinced her to go to the spa with her after Justine Monroe's call. Megan's toes and fingernails were freshly French manicured and her hair was straight down her back with loose curls on the ends. Her hairdresser added a few strawberry blonde highlights that matched her caramel skin and brought out her cheekbones.

Looking through her antique jewelry box, she picked a simple gold necklace and big gold hoops. When she was done, she surveyed her classy and elegant outfit in the full-length mirror. She looked like a senator's girlfriend should look, she thought.

Then she decided to lose the hoops and wear diamond studs instead. She didn't want to look too flashy and draw any more attention than necessary to herself. Megan was sure the attention would be on her more so than Steven when it came to the press. That was her only worry about agreeing to date Steven. While Megan was a people person at work, she really preferred privacy in her personal life. Megan laughed at herself as she realized that her private life was about to be flipped upside down.

After she was completely dressed, Megan added a little bit more makeup and sprayed on some Amarige. She looked at the grandfather clock that once belonged to her grandmother as she walked into the kitchen. She had a few more minutes, so she decided to drink a glass of cold water to calm her nerves even though a shot of whiskey would probably work better. While she was in the kitchen, her buzzer sounded. Let the games begin, she thought as she answered her intercom.

"Yes?"

"Hello, Megan. Are you ready to go?" It was Steven. She hadn't realized he would be picking her up. She assumed he was only sending a car. At least the driver would be in the car, she thought. But that wasn't good either. She would have to start pretending before the party, and she wasn't ready for that yet.

"Yes. Just surprised to hear your voice. I was expecting a driver."

"Change of plans. I'm driving."

Great. Now it will just be us together. I think I need that shot of whiskey now.

"Okay. I'll be down in a minute," Megan answered. She ran back into her bedroom and glanced in the mirror one last time. As she walked out the room, she said to Percy, "Wish me luck!" The cat just blinked and jumped on her bed. She knew he would stay there all night.

Megan grabbed her black evening purse and a shawl and headed down to the front lobby. When she arrived she saw Steven standing alone. He was on his cell and hadn't realized she was there. He looked handsome in a dark blue suit with a light blue dress shirt and a paisley tie. Megan's heart began to beat fast again, and her lips slightly parted as her stomach churned. As she watched him, she began to remember just how important a man he really was. He was a politician, a man with power and status. He was serious-minded. He had authority and a way of taking total command of any situation. Megan was impressed and it was a solid part of what made him one sexy man. Megan smiled when she realized that like her father, Steven spoke with his hands.

Steven was in a deep conversation with Bryce. He put his hand to his head in disbelief. Another main donor for the community center decided not to offer their usual amount for the summer program because of budget cuts with their company.

"Speak with Shawn and let him…" His voice trailed off. He knew Megan was behind him. He could smell her tantalizing perfume. He slowly turned and saw her sitting on one of the Victorian-style chairs in the lobby. She gave him an encouraging smile, and he took the phone away from his ear. He was pleased at her lovely appearance and for a quick second had forgotten why he was angry. Just looking at Megan sitting there so elegantly with her legs crossed wearing four-inch heels sent his mind on a journey to speechlessness.

Bryce was still talking, but Steven hadn't heard a single word. He had more important business to tend to at the moment. He regained his composure just long enough to get off of the phone.

"I gotta go, talk to Shawn. I'll see you fellas in about twenty minutes," he rather hurriedly told Bryce and pushed the end button on his cell phone screen. He rushed over to Megan as she stood up.

Megan took a deep breath as he approached her. She was suddenly feeling nervous and nauseous about the situation she placed herself in. *How can I play make-believe girlfriend for a handsome man that I could find myself falling for? No correction. That I am falling for.*

"You look beautiful," he said and kissed her on her cheek.

"Thank you. You look nice as well," she said, thinking the games had begun. She almost backed away when he kissed her cheek, but remembered that they were in public. She would later remind him however, only kisses on the cheeks and no lips. She could only imagine how his lips would kiss other places on her body.

"Ready?" he asked, holding out his hand. She put her hand into his, and they walked out to his car. He opened the passenger side of his black Mercedes convertible for her and she slid in, and he closed the door. When Steven got into the car, she noticed the strain on his face. As he started to drive, he stared straight ahead as a Sade CD played.

"Is everything okay?" she asked him. She was concerned. She wanted tonight to be special for him. There would be possible donors there as well as the media, and he had to put on his game face.

"Another donor that donates to the summer program backed out today." He glanced in her direction and then back on the road. "You know what I think?"

"That your reputation is beginning to catch up with you?"

"Yep. Bryce said the same statement earlier."

"Remember when I told you I may have some clients who may donate to the community center? They are coming tonight with checkbooks. Let me work my magic for you," she said patting his leg. As she tried to move her hand he grabbed it and held it tight.

"Thank you for supporting me, Megan." He held on to her hand until they pulled into the parking lot at the event. Before they got out of the car, Megan told him of her kissing rule. Steven agreed unless it was absolutely necessary. Megan gave him her "I don't think so look" as Steven drove the car to the front door for valet parking.

Once inside, Steven introduced Megan to his colleagues including Bryce and Shawn who both nodded approvingly. She gave a beautiful smile and said a lot of nice-to-meet-yous and thank-yous for coming to support Steven and the community center. She was glad when Tiffani, Syd and Jade arrived. They all gathered at Megan's table while Steven spoke with his guests.

"Girl, I'm so happy for you. You two look hot together!" Tiffani said with her cute dimples displaying on her smooth, sienna face.

"Yes, girl," Jade chimed in. "So glad you finally got a man and a wealthy one at that."

"I had a feeling there was something going on between you two," Sydney said. "You were just too giddy after he changed your tire. And the way you two were looking at each other all night at the gala, I just knew you would end up together. So happy for you, sis."

"Thank you. Now, if you ladies would excuse me, I need to go raise some money. Oh, and when I return please have your checks waiting," Megan said as she bounced away.

For the next hour, Megan indeed worked her magic with her clients that she invited including Chelsea and her husband, attorney Richard Benton, as well as a few others. Real-estate investor Broderick Hollingsworth was one of Megan's top clients. She had recently redone all of his rooms in a bed and breakfast he owned in Rome, Georgia. Because he trusted her judgment, he agreed to donate a large amount and offered a free weekend for her and Steven to relax at the inn. She thanked him for the free weekend although she knew they would never use it together. She would give it to Tiffani instead who could use a weekend away, and Megan would baby sit Keith Jr.—or KJ as he was affectionately called—considering he was her godson.

While she was speaking with Sharon Diamond, a romance author, she noticed Steven looking at her with the same strained look he had earlier. Megan wasn't sure why he appeared stressed, so she quickly ended her conversation with Sharon. Besides she already had her donation. She said thank you and walked over to Steven's side.

He was deep in a conversation with a gentleman who wasn't sure if he totally agreed with Steven's views on certain issues and said he was too wet behind the ears to run for his father's seat. She was about to walk away when Steven grabbed her hand and held on to it.

"Mr. Brown, this is Megan Chase, my girlfriend," Steven said. "Mr. Brown is one my father's colleagues."

"Nice to meet you, Mr. Brown. I'm sure you're as excited about Steven possibly running for the U.S. Senate as I am," she said warmly as she shook his hand looking him straight in the eyes. "Steven can you please be a dear and get me a bottled water. I'll stay and keep Mr. Brown company."

A few minutes later Steven returned with the bottled water as Mr. Brown and another gentleman who approached the conversation were writing checks and handing them to Megan.

"Steven, you've definitely found an angel. Where have you been hiding her? About time you settled down with *one* woman," Mr. Brown stated as he and the other older gentleman walked off to the buffet table.

"Ms. Chase, you've raised a lot of money for the community center. What have you been telling these people? You didn't make any promises I can't keep did you?" he asked teasingly.

"I told them you would give them your firstborn son if they donated." She paused to giggle. "I simply told them the truth. That you're the perfect candidate for the position and even though they might not agree with all of your political views, the children at the community center were more important than your political differences," she said, smiling up at him.

A sincere grin crossed his face. "Well, I certainly found the perfect candidate, as well. Oh, by the way, did you receive the flowers I sent earlier to your office?"

"Yes, I did. They were lovely. Thank you." She turned away. She didn't want him to see how truly happy she was about receiving the flowers. "Also, thank you for contacting Justine for me. She called today."

"She did?" he asked with a puzzled expression.

"Yes. She offered Jade and I a spot on the show this summer."

"Congratulations, except I never spoke to her."

Megan shook her head in disbelief. "Wait. What?"

"I called her and left a message, but I didn't tell her what it was about and she hasn't returned my call yet. Looks like you didn't need my help."

She smiled and then laughed. "Oh, my goodness. I'm shocked."

"Why? I saw your portfolio. You're a very talented and creative decorator. You deserve more than just a guest spot. You deserve your own show."

"Well that's the ultimate goal one day."

"Now, I know our agreement, but you aren't going to back out, are you?"

She shook her head and chuckled. "No, I want to help you clean up your image and help you win the seat." Megan stopped speaking as a reporter approached wanting to interview Steven about the community center and the rumor about him running for his father's seat. Megan left them to scout out Braxton who she hadn't had a chance to thank in person. She asked one of the waitresses who told her that he was downstairs. Megan peeked over the banister and saw her brother moving from table to table conversing with the patrons as the smooth sounds of the jazz band on the stage reverberated throughout the restaurant. She waved to get his attention, and he gave his charming smile that matched their father's. He jetted up the stairs as the group of women he had been speaking with checked him out. Megan didn't blame them. He was handsome in his dark gray suit that fit his muscular six-foot-four-inch frame. His bald head glistened under the dim lights, and Megan saw a few women fanning themselves. She shook her head and smiled as he approached and led her to an empty highboy table.

"Is everything set up how you wanted it?"

"Yes. Everything is perfect. Your staff did an awesome job. Are you playing tonight?"

"I may sit in with the band for a while but definitely on Friday and Saturday because my band is playing."

"I'm sure all of the women down there would love to hear you on the keys tonight."

"We'll see. So my baby sister is dating Senator Monroe. Have you told our parents? I can just hear Mother now."

"They don't know officially yet, but I'm sure they will by tomorrow."

He flashed a smile and Megan caught one of the waitresses looking his way blush. Her brother was indeed handsome with his perfectly trimmed mustache and goatee sitting on his chiseled, mocha face.

"Our mother will be calling you. I suggest you tell her first."

She simply nodded. Megan and her mother didn't always see eye to eye. She chatted with her brother for a few more minutes before one of the hostesses called him away.

"Hey," a deep voice said in her ear from behind her. "Having fun?" His lips skimmed the top of her ear causing her to feel faint. The emotions he made her experience in a split second were uncanny, and she needed to get out of there before she forgot they weren't really a couple and turned around to lay a juicy kiss on his inviting mouth.

She turned around slowly to face him. His handsome face no longer wore the tense expression from earlier. He looked more relaxed as he held a plate of appetizers in his hand. He dipped a shrimp into the cocktail sauce, popped the entire thing into his mouth and then ran his tongue along his bottom lip. It was such a seductive gesture that she knew she really needed to leave and quick.

"I believe the evening went well. I think we have received donations from most of the people here. I'm going to go home with Syd in a few minutes," Megan said, turning away from him to scan the room for Syd. She found her in a deep conversation with Bryce. Megan could only hope Syd wasn't telling him how she really felt about a case where Bryce had represented a man who the GBI had arrested. Syd had been certain the man was guilty although he was found not guilty. However, Bryce Monroe was one of Atlanta's top criminal attorneys and rarely lost a case.

"Oh, are you sure? The night is young, and we haven't even danced yet. Plus, if you think about it, this is our real first date since you refuse to count the lunch meeting," Steven said grabbing her hand as she turned back around to look at him. He placed his plate on the nearest table as the band began to play "Hello" by Lionel Richie.

"Well, luckily this is one of my favorite songs otherwise, I would say no," Megan said as he pulled her out onto the dance floor.

He placed her arms around his neck and his own hands around her waist.

"Are we putting on a show for the audience?" she

asked as her lips brushed against his ear by mistake. She felt him freeze for a second.

"Yes," he whispered back. They had plenty of spectators Megan noticed. *Good.* She'd made up her mind that evening that Steven would make an excellent U.S. senator. She intended to make sure that it happened, even if it meant slow dancing with him and holding his hand in public, which is something her ex never did when they were together. He didn't like public displays of affection. Even though Steven was just pretending, it still felt nice be in his warm embrace even if it was all one big lie.

The scent of his woodsy cologne whiffed into her nose. She wished it would rub off on her body so she could smell it later when she was alone in her bed. She wanted to dance with him for the rest of the evening but the song was almost over, and she hoped the band would play one more slow song so Steven would hold on to her just a little longer. She knew her brother was on the piano because she knew how he played that particular song. She tried to transfer her thoughts to him thinking that maybe he'd play one more slow song. She almost laughed at the idea but her and Sydney had their twin senses so maybe she could have it with Braxton, as well.

"Is my dancing that bad?" he whispered. "You're not smiling anymore."

She looked up at him with a smile. "Your dancing is on point."

"That's my girl," he said as he brushed the hair

over her ear that had fallen in her face. "What would you do if I kissed you right now?"

"Kiss you back and slap you later," Megan said seriously, while a heat wave rushed through her when he asked. She then found herself half wishing he would kiss her, but she knew it was all for show.

His smoldering gaze was seductive. Sexual. Dangerous.

Her breathing had become uneasy, and she suddenly became aroused, and she noticed he had, as well. She could feel his slight bulge against her pelvis area, and backed up a few inches. But he pulled her close again against his hard body. She began to wonder how it would be if they were naked and entangled in her sheets but quickly shook her head to clear her mind. Sexual tension was the last thing she wanted with Steven. He wanted to simply win the nomination, not her.

"That's a chance I'll have to take," he answered in a sexy, arrogant tone. He ran a finger alongside her cheek to her lips as they parted on command. He lowered his mouth to hers and caressed her lips with a slow, sensual kiss. A low moan escaped her throat as his tongue pushed deeper into her mouth, and she matched his seductive strokes in the same sweet rhythm.

Her hands journeyed up his neck and around to his face as he continued his passionate assault on her lips, showing no mercy. Not that she minded. In fact, she craved more than just a kiss and judging from the fervent groans he made, she could tell they were on the same page.

Megan was somewhat surprised he kissed her. She honestly didn't think he was serious, especially after she had threatened him with a slap in private. But she couldn't push him away with all of the people in the room thinking they were a couple. So of course she kissed him back. What else could she do as his pulsating tongue flicked along her bottom lip as if it belonged there? Every cell in her body was on an electrifying passionate ride that he was in control of.

He lifted his lips from hers as a protest cry escaped her mouth, and her eyes opened. Why on earth had he stopped? She could go on and on. Through the haze she was in, she could see Steven staring at her with a weird expression, and then she glanced around the room and saw all eyes on them as well as a few cheers and whistles.

"Everyone is staring," he said through a clenched smile. "Please don't slap me."

Remembering the premise of their relationship— for she had certainly forgotten for a moment—she smiled, as well. "Of course not. It's all for show."

"You think we were convincing enough? I saw a few shutterbugs, but I'm not sure. My eyes were closed, and I was too busy concentrating on your divine mouth."

"Good. You need the media to see you in a committed relationship and considering we've been in the blogs already, I'm sure tonight's pictures will have them convinced."

She knew she was convinced. Convinced she was falling for him. Hard. She tried to pull away from his embrace, but he placed a kiss on her forehead and slid his hands tenderly down her waist to her hips and finally off of her body. Megan rushed away from him and back over to where Sydney was sitting alone.

"Looks like someone is having a great time," Sydney said with a smirk.

"We were just kissing. So I saw you speaking to Bryce Monroe?" Megan said wanting to change the subject and get her mind off of the kiss.

"Yes, unfortunately. He's such an ass."

"He seems like a nice man." Megan glanced in his direction as he spoke with some of the guests. He was about the same height and build as Steven, except Bryce's hair was curlier and his complexion was more of a butterscotch shade. He had a strong jawline and a charismatic smile under a neatly trimmed mustache and goatee. He would make a great catch for someone.

"Not in the courtroom and definitely not with me." Sydney ran a hand through her bouncy bob.

"You ready to go, sissy?" Megan asked.

"I know I said I would take you home, but I just received a call from my partner. Big case and I need to head to the GBI office. I'm sure Steven can take you home. After all he did pick you up."

"But Syd…" Megan started. She didn't know if she could be alone with him again in the car especially after that crazy kiss that meant nothing to him and everything to her.

"Girl, you'll be fine. Just ask Steven now," Sydney said, nodding toward him.

Megan slowly turned around to find Steven directly behind her.

"Of course I can take you home, precious. Just give me a few minutes to say goodbye to Bryce and Shawn." He darted away before Megan could protest. Megan sat down with her lips pressed together.

"What's wrong with you? He is your man. Shouldn't he take you home?" Sydney inquired.

"Oh, sure. I just thought he needed to stay longer."

"The fund-raiser is pretty much over. Now, you know I'm the body language expert. I can tell that he is really into you and the way you almost galloped over here with that flushed face after your kiss, clearly suggests you want him, too. I thought surely you two were about to make love on the dance floor. So let him take you home and finish what he started," Sydney said.

"You sound like Jade."

"I'm just speaking the truth. Here he comes. Have a nice evening."

A few minutes later, Megan sat numbly in Steven's car fiddling with her purse. Luckily, Steven was on his cell phone talking to Shawn.

Megan stared out the window trying to concentrate on something else. Even though all she could manage to do was inhale his cologne and listen to his deep voice. She had no idea what he was saying but the angrier he became the sexier he became, and her mind kept travelling back to the kiss.

She stole glances at him wondering how long she could keep up this charade that she wasn't really attracted to him. She was becoming highly upset at the fact that he had been on the phone the entire time, which made it clear he had no interest in her. Megan shook her head angrily and then gave him an ice-cold glare. She couldn't believe she thought that kiss could've meant something to him, as well.

When they arrived at her parking garage, Steven was still on the phone in a deep conversation with Shawn. Megan reached to open her door, but Steven placed his hand on her arm and shook his head. Megan looked at him and realized his facial expression was one of annoyance but not for her.

"Shawn, I can't keep going over and over on this issue with you. You know my view and it's not going to change. So let's just drop it." Steven breathed heavily and hung up his phone without saying goodbye. Keeping his hand on her arm, he loosened his grip and then rested his head back on his seat. He turned to face Megan.

"I apologize for being on the phone and ignoring you. Trust me that wasn't my intention, baby. Shawn can be so…what's the word…?"

"Annoying?" Megan asked, feeling a little better that he wasn't trying to ignore her. Did he just say *baby?*

"Something like that. He keeps trying to change my mind about certain things. He's not in my shoes and doesn't understand the pressures politicians have to face. I'm sorry for complaining to you. I know you probably don't want to hear me babble about my political stuff."

"That's what girlfriends are for right? To listen and support their man?" Megan said, teasingly and punching him lightly on the shoulder.

Steven smiled at her comment. "I'm beginning to think perhaps that's what they're for." He chuckled and patted her hand. "I forgot to tell you thank you for tonight. You really did work your magic," he said touching her face tenderly with his hand. He moved closer to her and pulled her face close to his, resting his head on her forehead.

"Just one more little kiss?" he asked in a sexy voice that sent a tremble through her body.

"But…" Megan started.

"But what? Didn't we have a good time on our first date?"

"It wasn't a date."

"So you didn't feel anything with that kiss on the dance floor?"

"No." She couldn't tell him the truth. The last thing she wanted to do was to get caught up in a fairy tale that she knew would end sooner for him than it would for her.

He slid back to his side. "Well, let me walk you up to your loft," he said seemingly taken aback.

"I can manage by myself," she said, opening the door and stepping out of the car. He got out and pushed the remote to lock the car.

"I said I would walk with you, Ms. Chase."

"Ms. Chase? I thought we were on first name basis, Stevo," she said, giving him a sincere smile. However, he remained silent. She continued to walk ahead of him to the elevator. They remained quiet on the ride up and when they got off, he continued to follow her to her door. Megan unlocked it, but she didn't open it. She turned to face Steven and smiled at him. She stood on her tippy toes and reached up to kiss him lightly on the cheek.

"Good night, Steven. I had a lovely time on our first date."

Megan went inside and leaned her back against the door. *Boy, that was close,* she thought as Percy greeted her by rubbing around her legs.

"How did I ever get myself into this mess?" she asked herself out loud, picking up the cat and walking toward her bathroom to take a refreshing shower. Steven Monroe was making her feel things she had never felt before. She just hoped she could get through the next few months without completely falling in love with him.

Chapter 6

A week had passed since Megan had seen Steven but she'd spoken to him a few times while he was out of town. Their relationship was growing into a comfortable friendship that she pleasantly enjoyed. She was genuinely concerned about his senatorial duties, and she could tell that he loved to hear her opinions. Although politics had never sparked an interest in her before, she was up all night reading his platform, speeches and emailing him her thoughts.

The day after the fund-raiser, tons of pictures hit the internet on gossip blogs, Twitter, Instagram and Facebook. However, there was one she couldn't get out of her mind. *The kiss.* It had been snapped from so many different angles that there were at least twenty different pictures, but they all conveyed the same thing. That the senator was finally in love and had tossed aside his playboy ways for her. Of course that's what they wanted the media to think. Unfortunately when she looked at the pictures, she saw herself falling in love with a man that would never want her in that way. Sure, she figured he was attracted to her, and she sensed he wanted her but more than likely only for sex. Since it was Friday, she decided to work from home instead of going into the office. She'd brought home the duvet, toss pillows and shams she was working on for Chelsea, but Megan wasn't in the mood to work. Her thoughts were still on last Thursday night at the fund-raiser. Dancing with Steven felt nice. It had been a long time since a man made her feel special. It reminded her that she would find love again and that all men weren't like her ex.

She glanced at the clock. It was a quarter to seven. She got up and walked across the room to turn off the alarm that would sound in a few minutes. She wasn't in the mood to jog on the treadmill, so she opted to do one hundred stomach crunches on her yoga mat.

Afterward, Megan walked barefoot to the kitchen with Percy following closely behind her. He was hungry, otherwise he would still be on her bed. She took out his food and noticed the roses and tulips on her island. They still looked beautiful even after a week, and she hoped they would stay alive for just a little while longer. It had been a long time since she had flowers in her home that she hadn't bought for herself.

After giving Percy his food, Megan decided that

a cup of coffee followed by thirty minutes of yoga and meditation would help her relax. While she was rinsing out her coffee pot, her phone rang, and she already knew who it was. Her dad was the only person who would call this early in the morning. He was always at his school by six-thirty to make sure he had everything in order for the day.

Megan had been avoiding her parents. Her mother had left a very distraught voice mail yesterday about her dating Steven. But she finally decided she might as well get it over with and speak to her dad. He was more understanding. Megan didn't bother looking at the caller ID as she answered the phone.

"Hello, Daddy," Megan sighed.

"Daddy? I thought my nickname was Stevo, but I can get used to Daddy. How about Big Daddy? Big Poppa? S. Diddy, you know, like P. Diddy? No wait, it's just Diddy now." He paused, but continued when she remained silent. "Well, I was hoping to get a laugh or a smile from you this morning."

"Steven, I thought you were my father!" Megan said embarrassed. "He's the only person to ever call me this early."

"I wanted to catch you before you went to work."

"I took the day off, but I still have a project to finish and an appointment this afternoon with a potential donor for the community center." Megan walked to the kitchen table to double-check her schedule on her tablet.

"I have to go to Washington, D.C., today. I wanted to know if you could go with me."

"I didn't know I would have to travel," she said, wrinkling her brow.

"I know its short notice, but I have a black-tie charity function to attend on Saturday night that I hadn't planned on going to, but Shawn is insisting I go. Other congressmen and senators will be there with their wives and girlfriends. I thought it would look nice to have you on my arm. You can fly out on the private plane that Bryce and I share."

Private plane?

"I see. When are we returning?"

"You could come back on Sunday or Monday. But I have to stay for some meetings, so I'll return on Wednesday."

"Steven, this is such short notice. I don't have anything to wear to a fancy function in Washington, D.C.," Megan said truthfully.

"I knew you would say something like that. That's why I arranged for you to go shopping with Chelsea today at Barneys. She's already in New York City meeting with some other clients."

"But I have an appointment at two with an executive from Coke about donating to the community center."

"Shawn can go. What other excuses are you going to come up with?"

"What time are we leaving? I have to finish a project," Megan said reluctantly. She couldn't believe she agreed to go with him to Washington, D.C.

"I've arranged for the plane to take you to New York City this morning and then to D.C. once you're done shopping. I have a function to attend this evening in Atlanta so I'll meet you later on tonight. I'm sending a car to take you to the airfield around ten, so get to packing."

"I don't have Barney's money," Megan answered, thinking about what she had in her closet to wear.

"But I do." Without another word, he hung up.

Three hours later Megan was in the limo headed to a private airfield that she didn't know existed in Atlanta. Since her conversation with Steven earlier that morning, she managed to finish her project, pack and drop Percy off at Tiffani's. Megan also had the misfortune of answering the phone without looking at the caller ID while packing. When she heard her mother's voice, Megan cursed in silence and hoped the conversation wouldn't last long.

Her mother wasn't happy about her daughter flying to Washington with someone that she hadn't met yet. She told Megan about her research on Senator Monroe and that she wasn't at all thrilled with the results. Her teacher friends even told her to tell Megan to be careful.

"Megan, it's not a good idea to date him. He doesn't care for you. You just got out of a long term relationship," Mrs. Chase fussed. "You're very vulnerable right now. Men feed off of that! Men like him love that! There is no challenge for him, and he's going to just use you and then throw you away like all of the others!"

"Mother, you don't know what you're talking about. Everything is fine. I'm not trying to start a serious relationship now. We're just dating. That's all!" Megan threw her clothes into the suitcase instead of folding them. Megan and her mother never saw eye to eye, and most of their conversations usually ended because of disagreements.

"Dating? It seems as if you're flying out of town with him! I hardly call that dating! He just wants to have sex with you and then move on to some other pretty young thang!"

"Mother!"

"Megan, you're my daughter. I love you. I'm only looking out for your best interests. And dating a senator, especially one like Steven Monroe, isn't just a regular relationship, honey." Her mother paused and was silent for moment. Megan hated that. She knew that meant her mother's mind was churning for more reasons as to why she shouldn't date Steven.

"Mother..." Megan started before she continued.

"Everyone will know. You'll be on television, in the tabloids. Your life will no longer be private. This is so embarrassing!"

"Embarrassing for whom? You? Are you scared of what your teacher friends will say to you or what they've already said to you? Mother, I'm a grown woman, in case you've forgotten. I know what I'm doing. Steven is a nice guy. Now I have to go finish packing. I love you, Mom." She then hung up before her mother could bicker more.

Megan decided to call her dad on the way to the private airport. It was easier to call him at work when she knew her mother wouldn't be around to snatch the phone and voice her opinion some more. She spoke to her father briefly in between him suspending two boys for fighting.

"How did you meet him? Isn't he out of your circle? Is this Syd's doing?" Dr. Chase sounded concerned. Megan had always been daddy's little girl, and she understood that her father didn't want to see his daughter hurt again by yet another man.

"We're just trying to get to know each other. It's not that serious," Megan told her father.

"Does he play golf? I'm sure he does."

"I think so, Dad," Megan answered making a mental note to ask him.

"When do I meet him? I have some political and personal questions for him."

"Soon, Dad. I'm going to Washington with him for a function this weekend. Maybe next weekend." She had no intentions of introducing them. She doubted Steven wanted to meet her parents.

"Your mother called earlier ranting. You just be careful. You know how those politicians are, and he's a playboy."

"People change, Dad."

"Yeah, and you said that about that punk ex-boyfriend of yours. He was too arrogant and only concerned about his status and not loving and taking care of my baby girl. You know I never liked him."

"Yes, Daddy, I know. Well, I'm going to let you get back to running your school," Megan said trying to get off of the phone. Once her dad got started on a tirade, he didn't know how to stop.

"I have some teacher evaluations to do this morning, so yes I need to go."

"I'm sure they're looking forward to seeing you arrive unannounced." Megan was glad she decided not to become a teacher. She loved being her own boss and not having to worry about someone always looking over her shoulder.

When Megan boarded the private jet, she was greeted by a flight attendant. The woman held out her delicate, manicured hand to shake Megan's.

"Good morning, Ms. Chase. I'm Susan, and I'll be your flight attendant for today. Senator Monroe has informed me to take extra special care of you. Would you like a mimosa while I give you a tour?" Susan stepped aside to let Megan walk in front of her.

Megan stood in awe. The main cabin of the jet had six plush, oversize white leather chairs on top of a very beautiful gold-and-white Persian carpet. She was used to flying coach or sometimes business class, but the Monroe family jet represented accommodations seen only in illustrious magazines.

"No thank you to the mimosa, but a definite yes to the tour. This is absolutely breathtaking." She looked at Susan. "I bet you love your job!" Megan exclaimed as Susan began to show her around. In the cockpit, she made a quick introduction of Captain Simmons.

The jet was about twice the size of a motor mansion, with the same luxuries, including a mini-kitchen, wet bar, a bedroom, and a bathroom in the back of the plane.

Megan walked back to the front. She hated taking trips on a plane and preferred to be asleep during the flight. Especially the last twenty minutes because her ears would always clog up, and she wouldn't be able to hear that well for at least three hours afterward. She'd brought a bag of jellybeans and a pack of gum to snack on to prevent excessive ear clogging

She decided to sit up front in one of the reclining seats and have a glass of orange juice from the wet bar to accompany the breakfast that Susan served. Captain Simmons informed Megan that there was a thirty-minute delay because they had to wait for a clear runway at the small airport. While Megan enjoyed her breakfast of French toast, shrimp and grits, and a spinach-and-feta-cheese omelet, she was interrupted by her cell phone ringing.

"Hello?"

"Hey, I called to check on you," Steven said.

"I'm fine. I'm eating a delicious breakfast."

"Shrimp and grits?"

"Yep, and it's so good. We're taking off in a few minutes."

"I have a meeting and then a fitting for my tux to wear on Saturday. My housekeeper Greta will pick you up from the airport."

"Oh. I didn't know you had a housekeeper."

"Greta is a sweetheart. She's been with the Monroe family since I was born. She's almost like a second mom to me and my siblings. By the way, I may not be in Washington until after midnight, so don't wait up." He hesitated for moment and cleared his throat. "Megan, I need to prewarn you. Greta is expecting you to sleep in the master bedroom."

"Wait! I can't sleep in the same bed with you," she said aloud, but then remembering she wasn't alone, Megan lowered her voice. "I'm sure your brownstone has a guest room!"

"It does, but Greta also knows me, and my female guests have never slept in the guest room. Don't worry, I have a California King bed. You won't know I'm there."

"Fine! Stay on your side!"

Once Megan arrived to New York, she met Chelsea in Manhattan. Chelsea had arranged with Barneys and a few other places for Megan to try on and purchase a dress for the evening.

Chelsea spoke on her cell phone a mile a minute, speaking in her usual "I'm in control and don't you forget it" tone. She smiled and winked at Megan while they walked down 5th Avenue.

Megan walked alongside her mentor, thinking about the upcoming weekend and what her father said earlier, even though Chelsea's conversation was much more interesting. Megan had always admired Chelsea since her mother had first introduced them at a sorority meet-and-mingle tea. The two of them immediately developed a mentor and mentee bond. She admired Chelsea for her wit, sassiness and for always knowing the right thing to say in any situation. She was truly fabulous at fifty with her pixie cut hairstyle, size six frame, and stunning appearance that always turned heads.

Chelsea was currently using her wit and sassiness to appease an irate client. She talked and walked fast in her Louboutin's as if they were tennis shoes. Megan increased her pace in her flat gladiator sandals in order to keep up.

"*Chérie,* my love. The awards show is a month away. I have already spoken to someone at Versace, and they're making five one-of-a-kind evening gowns just for you to try on." Chelsea paused and rolled her eyes, which made Megan giggle silently. "No one else will have the same dress. My assistant has already spoken to a rep from Harry Winston about a diamond choker with matching earrings. Have I ever let you down?" Chelsea shook her head at Megan. "Of course not, my love. Now go finish recording that number one song and let me handle the big things," Chelsea said before her client could oppose. She pushed the off button on her phone.

"Girl, these celebrities never know what they want. That's why they hire me to tell them." Chelsea tossed her phone into her purse and placed her aviator shades in her hair as they walked into Barney's.

Megan nodded her head in agreement.

"I understand completely. I have a celebrity client right now who keeps changing her mind about what type of rug she wants in front of her fireplace. Her home is being featured in a magazine next month, and she's a nervous wreck, which is driving me crazy. However, I'm excited that one of my creations will be in *House to Home Magazine*. Now if my client will just make up her mind before the photo shoot." Normally Megan made all of the decisions, but this particular celebrity client wanted to give her two cents. Luckily, Lucy was going to handle the rug problem on Monday.

"Probably the same person," Chelsea said. "Now let's get back to why we're here. You need an evening dress for a black-tie function. There're some gowns that I want you to try on as well as some other things."

"Other things?"

"I've already called ahead and had the saleslady take out several black gowns in a size six for you to try on," Chelsea continued as Megan looked at her questionably.

"But what other things?"

"I was thinking since you're dating Senator Monroe, you may want to invest in getting a few more items. Some suits, cute sundresses for the summer. No shorts or minis. Some nice summer slacks and blouses. I know you're only twenty-six, but we're going to have to get rid of the baby doll and peasant top look you've been wearing since college. No more Gap and Old Navy, my love," Chelsea said glancing at Megan's T-shirt and bootcut jeans.

"Chelsea, I'm only here to buy a dress," Megan complained not interested in an image makeover.

"Correction, Mr. Monroe is going to buy the dress and whatever else you want. He gave me a limit and trust me it's a nice one because there isn't one. It will all be charged to his Black Card. A whole new wardrobe for the summer. We'll do the fall one when the time comes. He said that personally. I guess his bachelor days are over with!" Chelsea said looking through a rack of sundresses, pulling out several and handing them to the saleslady. Chelsea continued while the brightness in Megan's face slowly faded.

"Next week I'm going to go through your closet and tag the clothes you're not to wear while out with him just in case you get photographed. What wife of a senator do you know that dresses like you? Sweetie, you dress really cute but remember you're dating a senator now."

"I'm not married to him, Chelsea."

"Not yet, my love. Not yet. And of course I'll help you pick out your wedding gowns. You must have one for the ceremony and another for the reception. I'm sure Vera will design something special just for you. Then you'll need a whole new wardrobe as a married woman. We can store your old clothes in your guest room closet or give them to charity. I'm sure you can use the tax write-off."

"Chelsea, let's go through my closet first before we begin buying other things. I own a lot of nice suits and dresses. I have to wear jeans and sweats when I'm doing a job. I have to be comfortable if I'm on a ladder painting, moving furniture or hanging wallpaper."

"Sweetheart, I'm only following orders from Mr. Monroe. He is paying me nicely to select clothes for you. Now, my goal is to give you a new look and style of your own. We want other politicians' wives, girlfriends and even their mistresses to be jealous of you plus set out a new trend. Remember Jackie O?" Chelsea inquired placing a dozen of dresses on the chair next to Megan and going back for more.

"The rapper?" Megan asked sarcastically.

"You know exactly who I mean. First Lady Jacqueline Kennedy Onassis. Her style was graceful, elegant and classy. Everyone wanted to look like her, dress like her. People still admire her sense of style and poise. That's what I want for you. I want people to see a sophisticated young lady on the arm of Senator Monroe. Do you understand, honey?" Chelsea asked seriously.

Megan groaned as she took several dresses into the dressing room. For the next three hours she tried on more outfits than she had that entire year. She tried to suck it up and have fun, but all she could think about was sleeping next to Steven that night and hoped she wouldn't have the urge to seduce him.

Chapter 7

Megan arrived in Washington, D.C., around eight in the evening. Her ears had finally regained most of their hearing as she stepped off of the plane, chewing her fourth piece of gum. She looked around and saw an older, kind-looking lady holding a sign that read Megan Chase in bold letters. She waved at the woman, who she assumed to be Greta, and walked hurriedly over to her.

"Good evening, Ms. Chase. I'm Greta Reid, Senator Monroe's housekeeper. Your bags are being put into the car. Do you need anything before we go to the house?" Greta had a Southern accent, a grandmotherly presence and a genuine smile. Her gray hair was in fresh curls around her warm, brown face and her pleasant demeanor made Megan comfortable.

"No, and it's very nice to meet you," Megan said, shaking Greta's hand. Greta looked rather surprised when Megan took her hand.

"Now, Ms. Chase..." Greta began.

"Please, call me Megan."

"All right, Ms. Megan. Is there anything you do or don't want to eat for breakfast in the morning? I can cook just about anything from A to Z, at least that's what the Monroe family says."

"No, whatever you cook is fine with me just as long as coffee goes with it." Megan enjoyed eating a hearty breakfast when possible, and she could sense that Ms. Greta seemed like the type to cook big meals.

"Well, I haven't seen Mr. Steven for almost a month, so I'm going to fix all of his favorites," Greta said as they walked to the car.

"If you need any help, let me know."

"Ms. Megan, that's sweet of you, but you just enjoy yourself these next few days. Mr. Steven said you're a hard-working interior decorator. I'm sure you can use the break."

"Do you have any children?" Megan asked.

"I have two daughters. Both married with kids. They live in Mobile, Alabama. That's where I'm originally from. I'm usually there until Mr. Steven calls me a few days before he arrives here in Washington or in Savannah. Mr. Steven is like the son I never had as well as Mr. Bryce," Greta said as they approached the car. It was a black Lexus LS 460.

"You don't live here all the time?"

"No, Ms. Megan. I'm sort of on call for Mr. Steven or anyone else in the Monroe family. I'm retired now. I've worked for the Monroe family for many years. Changed all of the Monroe children's dirty diapers."

"Well, you're a part of the family. Do you travel with him sometimes?"

"Sometimes, but Mr. Steven is a simple guy, if you can believe that. He knows how to cook and clean for himself, even though I spent most of the day cleaning." Greta opened the back door for Megan. "He said he wanted it to be perfect for you and now I see why."

"Ms. Greta, I'm not used to having people chauffeur me around. Can I sit up front with you?"

"Of course, sugar. You know, you're different from those uppity girls I see him with in the newspapers and magazines. When he used to bring them here or to Savannah, they wouldn't even acknowledge my presence. I think he has a keeper now." Greta winked.

When they arrived at the brownstone, Greta told Megan to make herself at home. It was a beautiful, three-story building with a studio apartment on the top floor that Greta mentioned she stayed in when she was there. The masculine decorations reminded her of Steven. Sturdy, strong furniture in dark colors. Greta took her up to the second floor to the master suite. It was a large room with a sitting area with a fireplace, and two big, brown-leather, comfy-looking chairs and an oversize leather ottoman. The bed was huge with cherrywood posts. It was so high off the ground it had matching steps on both sides.

"Right around the corner is your closet. I've already put away your things for you while you toured the brownstone. What a stunning dress you're wearing tomorrow evening. I'll steam it for you before you put it on tomorrow. It got a few wrinkles from the plane ride. You know those baggage handlers just throw people's stuff around."

"Thank you so much, Ms. Greta," Megan said thinking there was a "his" closet on the other side of the master bathroom. The one that was supposed to be "hers" was empty except for her things, a few African paintings, and a stack of about a dozen books sitting on the floor.

After Megan ate a delicious Southern dinner of chicken fried steak, mashed sweet potatoes and collard greens, she retired back upstairs to the bedroom and looked through the books that were on the floor in the closet. Reading was her favorite pastime. She found a Walter Mosley novel that she hadn't read yet and quickly read through the first few chapters in one of the big comfy chairs in the sitting area. She found herself yawning an hour later and decided to get up and walk around. She went into the master bath, which was an interior decorator's dream. A beautiful antique tub with four brass legs stood in the middle. The floor and countertops were marble. There were two vanities on opposite walls. The "hers" vanity had a makeup area with a timeless antique chair. There was a shower big enough for two.

Now that Megan was on her feet, she realized how exhausted she was. She decided to take a warm shower and climb into bed. Then it hit her again that she would be sleeping in the same bed as Steven. She'd almost forgotten. But he was right about one thing—it was an enormous bed.

After a refreshing shower, she walked into the bedroom, wrapped in her towel. She remembered Greta telling her she would put her nightclothes on the bed for her. When Megan walked into the room, the sheets on the right side were pulled back, but she didn't see her pajamas on the bed. Instead, Greta had laid out the little black slip that was in the same garment bag as her evening gown.

"Ha," Megan said out loud, walking to the closet with the slip to find the pajamas. She didn't see them anywhere. She knew she packed them.

"I was on the phone arguing with my mother, packing my suitcase. I folded up the shirt…" Megan realized that the pajamas were still lying on her bed in Atlanta. *What am I going to wear to bed?* Her only other choice was her workout clothes. *They will have to do.* She slipped on a tank top and pink velour shorts. The shorts had shrunk somewhat when she last washed them, but it was better than wearing the slinky black slip. She didn't want to give Steven any ideas.

Satisfied, Megan walked back into the room, only to discover Steven asleep in one of the leather chairs by the fireplace. Time flew, she thought. It was only midnight. She had planned on being asleep when he arrived.

She stopped abruptly in the doorway and stared at him. He sat somewhat slumped down in the chair with his legs apart. His hand rested on his forehead as if he had a headache. A loosened tie hung around his neck, and the first few buttons on his shirt were undone to reveal a glimpse of his smooth chest. Megan had the urge to straddle his lap and wind her arms around his neck and run her tongue down his skin. She shook her head at the thought and began to walk toward the bed, but the hardwood floor creaked, and his eyes flew open. He smiled and sat up straight.

"You're here early," she said, feeling awkward. She didn't know if she should climb into the bed or not.

"Yep. I was able to leave the gathering earlier than planned. Have you found everything you needed?" He began to unbutton his sleeve cuffs.

"Yes, thank you. Greta is wonderful." Megan decided to sit in the other chair across from him. "These are really cozy chairs," she said, rubbing her hands on the arms of the chair to feel the texture of the leather.

"Thank you. I just bought them and had them delivered when Greta got here. I used to have an old couch sitting here. When I saw these chairs in a magazine, I knew they would look nice by the fireplace. Greta did a good job picking out the comforter on my new bed." Steven looked admiringly at the gold-and-red comforter.

"New bed?" She was rather relieved that no other woman had slept in it. *But why should that matter? It's not as if we're a couple.*

"Yes, I ordered it at the same time as the chairs. I used to have a queen sleigh bed in here, but I had it moved to an empty room down the hall. I needed a change." He walked over and ran his hand over the comforter. "I haven't even slept in it yet, and now I can't wait especially since I get to share it with a sexy lady."

"Watch yourself, Steven. You better stay on your side of the bed."

"I promise. Scout's honor. Did you enjoy your shopping spree today?" He hopped up and sat on the bed. His longs legs barely touched the hardwood floor.

"Yes, I did. Thank you. Chelsea knows what she's doing. I also picked out a really nice tie for you, as well. Maybe you can wear it on Election Day," Megan suggested. "I hung it in your closet."

"Thank you. So you just know I'm going to win the primaries and then make it to November's election?"

"Of course. I've read the information about the other potential candidates vying for your father's seat. And I'm not saying this because I know you, but I really do think you're the best candidate. The only thing that may have been holding you back was your lifestyle. But the media loves that you've settled down… Well…sort of, I suppose. So, yes, I think you have a pretty good chance of winning."

"Megan, you keep blowing my head up like this, and I'll never let you go," he said in a sexy tone that caused her breathing to pause for a second and a sensual warmth rushed over her skin.

A heated, seductive stare passed between them and for a moment, Megan wished what he said would really happen, but she couldn't dwell on that. They were simply two people helping each other obtain their career goals. The media was finally warming up to him, and she'd seen a boost of phone calls from prospective clients after the event at Braxton's restaurant. Besides, she enjoyed her freedom of being single and so did Steven. After the election, they could return to their normal lives. But would it be normal or miserable because he would no longer be a part of her life?

"Well…I'm going to go take a shower," Steven said as he strode into the bathroom and closed the door.

Megan wasn't sure what to do next. She decided to get in the bed and try to fall asleep before he returned. If she wasn't, she would pretend she was sleep. She looked around the room again before getting under the covers. Greta had indeed done a wonderful job. Now all that was needed were new curtains and a few throw rugs on the hardwood floor and the bedroom would be complete. She thought of all of this as she drifted off to sleep between the fresh Egyptian cotton sheets.

Steven let the warm water from the shower wash over his tired body. He could still smell her scent in the shower, and it continued to arouse him. When he woke up to find Megan in a tank top and her very short shorts, he found himself at a loss of words. The way the shorts fit around her hips and bottom made him very happy to be a man. He couldn't believe he managed to talk about comforter sets and furniture. What he wanted was to run his hands on her smooth, freshly oiled legs and taste the scent that emanated from her body when she walked causally into the room and sat in the chair next to him. Even though she wasn't wearing lingerie, she was still sexy with her pink shorts and her hair pinned up on her head. He had to quickly escape to the bathroom so she wouldn't see his growing erection.

After his refreshing shower, Steven went back into the bedroom. He glanced over to the bed. He didn't want to make her any more uncomfortable than she already was, so he decided to sleep on the old couch in his spacious walk-in closet. Plus, he was still aroused and couldn't handle sleeping next to her without touching her. He watched her sleep for a moment before he turned off the lamp on the nightstand.

Saturday evening the celebrity stylist Chelsea had arranged to do Megan's hair and makeup, clapped his hands excitedly as Megan turned around twice so he could admire his creation.

"Girlfriend, you are absolutely fierce! You're going to make heads turn!" Keenan the stylist said admiringly, snapping two fingers in the air. "Especially the senator's."

Megan smiled at herself in the floor-length mirror on the wall in the foyer. Her long hair was piled up in a flowy updo with long, curly strands framing her face. Her makeup was light and flawless. Her straight black dress with a lace overlay hit her curves in all the right places, highlighting her curvy hips and small waist. The salesman at Barney's told her and Chelsea that no one else was able to really fill out the dress like Megan, including a lot of celebrities who had tried on the dress and didn't look as good as she did. Megan thought the guy was probably just trying to sell it and would say anything so she would buy it.

"Thank you so much, Keenan! I wish I could take you back to Atlanta." Megan gave him a hug and then a kiss on each cheek.

"Chile, please! When Senator Monroe wins the U.S. Senate seat, I'm sure I'll see you more often in D.C. Here's my card." Keenan handed her his business card and then turned toward the staircase to retrieve his styling materials from upstairs. "I'm sure you and the senator will be attending more functions in Washington for years to come." He ran into Steven on the first landing.

"Senator Monroe, it took me hours to do her hair. Please don't ruin it tonight after the event, but if you did, I wouldn't blame you. She looks ravishing, but don't tell my boyfriend I said that."

Megan gazed at Steven as he descended the stairs, still laughing about Keenan's comments. She was so glad to see him that she almost ran and jumped into his arms. But instead she stood still, her heels pressed into the hardwood floor. She hadn't seen him since he went to take a shower, and she fell straight to sleep after a long day. She woke up in the middle of the night to the realization that he wasn't next to her in the bed. At first she was relieved that he'd chosen to sleep elsewhere and then slightly disappointed. After he'd called her sexy, she was sort of hoping that he would just go ahead and seduce her. When she woke up, there was a note on what would've been his pillow stating he wouldn't be at breakfast and was going to play golf but that he arranged a day of pampering for her at the spa. Megan was relieved. She didn't want to play the devoted girlfriend around Greta. However, Greta was disappointed because she had made all of his favorite breakfast dishes.

Steven stopped on the last stair and a debonair smile inched across his face before he stepped into her personal space.

"You look absolutely lovely."

Warmth dissipated all over her body, and she couldn't help but offer a gracious smile. "Thank you and you look as if you just stepped out of *GQ Magazine*," she said as her eyes perused over his attire. He wore a black Armani tux with a cravat instead of a bowtie. His diamond cuff links sparkled.

He was indeed an exquisite-looking man. Megan felt overwhelmed to have such an amazing man as her escort. She just hoped she could get through the evening without ripping his clothes off. The way he stared at her made her feel sexy and wanted. He stepped closer toward her with a smoldering gaze, and her heart began to beat uncontrollably as his hand reached out to slide the hair out of her face.

"You're so beautiful." His voice was barely above a whisper.

Greta rushed into the foyer with a camera. Steven stepped away from Megan, and she turned to grab her purse from the credenza. She was relieved Greta came into the room. One more second and Steven's lips would be on hers. It was a chance she couldn't take. She knew just one more kiss from him would send her over the edge, and they would never make it to the Smithsonian.

"Oh, just look at my babies. Now let me get a few pictures of the two of you," Greta said, holding up her digital camera, pulling Megan and Steven to each other.

Megan felt as if she was going to her high school prom again, and her mother was making a big fuss. Except this time her date didn't look scared stiff because of the prom-rules talk with her father moments before. Steven and Megan scooted together and posed for several pictures. Greta beamed with sheer delight. Megan glanced at Steven, who seemed to be enjoying the photo session, too.

Steven was surprised at Greta's actions. In all his years of going to functions with women, including his ex-wife, Greta had never gone to this extent of being concerned about his dates. The most Greta would say was "have a nice evening, sir" and hand him his trench coat.

"Have a great time," Greta said opening the front door. "Are you sure you don't need me to drive you?"

"No. This event may not end until late. Just get some rest. I want all of my favorites in the morning." Steven chuckled and gave Greta a kiss on her cheek. "I promise, no golfing." He grabbed Megan's hand and squeezed it gently as they walked to the car.

"You seem nervous," Steven said once they were in the car headed to the Smithsonian. He didn't want her to feel out of place this evening. He knew she wasn't used to this type of event. However, because she was such an elegant and classy lady, he knew she would be able to handle herself with the other girlfriends and wives.

"Just a little. I've been to numerous events but never a dinner fund-raiser where the plates were $500.00 each. I don't spend that much in one month on groceries!"

"Yeah, the price is quite steep, but the money raised is going to the Save the Manatee campaign in Florida. They're slowly becoming extinct." He had a soft spot for the huge animals that were being killed by ships and boats.

"Hmm, interesting. I saw recently on a documentary that the propellers on the boats are striking them, leaving scars, or even worse, causing their death. That's so sad. I'm glad to see how concerned you are about the manatees."

"I'm an animal lover."

Steven tried to stare straight ahead but his eyes kept wandering to the beauty sitting next to him. Keenan was right. She was indeed ravishing, and it took everything in him not to pull the car over and mess up her hair. However, it was clear to him that Megan wasn't interested in being anything more than friends or at least she didn't want to admit to it.

Moments later, they arrived at the Smithsonian. There were cameras flashing as they walked the red carpet, and they stopped and posed for a few pictures before going inside.

He squeezed her hand. "Don't be nervous," he reassured her as they walked into the event. "I'm by your side."

After the hostess showed them to their table, they were offered a choice of wines. They both opted for an iced tea and lemonade instead. Some other politicians and their wives or girlfriends joined their table of ten. The men mostly talked about politics, sports and the president while the women discussed fashion and what clothes they were taking on their upcoming fabulous vacations. Steven could tell that Megan was trying really hard to join the conversation, but all of the women were so superficial. Megan was down-to-earth and not concerned with such nonsense.

"So where are you two vacationing this summer, Megan?" Mrs. Douglas, the wife of U.S. Senator Richard Douglas from Nevada, asked. He was one of Steven's golfing buddies from that morning.

"Not really sure. I have a lot of work to do this

summer." Megan glanced at Steven with a "help me" look on her face.

"What do you do besides look tenderly at Senator Monroe?" Mrs. Douglas asked.

Steven smiled at Mrs. Douglas's comment. If she thought Megan was looking tenderly at him, then she must've been doing a good job of faking it.

"I have my own interior-design business in Atlanta. This summer I'm doing a show for the Fabulous Living Channel as well as still finding time to spend with my Steven."

"Splendid! You two have to come to our place in the Hamptons this summer." Mrs. Douglas placed her hand on her forehead. "Megan, I'm in dire need of redoing some of the guest rooms and bathrooms there. Maybe you can give me some suggestions or better yet, just do it for me." Mrs. Douglas scooted closer to Megan.

"I'll have to check my schedule, but I'm sure a few days at your summer home would be lovely, Mrs. Douglas," Megan answered sincerely. "And I'd be happy to help you with your decorating needs."

After dessert, Steven and Megan said their goodbyes. He could see the relief on her face when he announced they were leaving. As they walked to the door, he heard someone call his name in a familiar tone.

"Senator Monroe," a woman called after him. Steven cringed before he turned around. He knew that voice in his sleep. It belonged to his ex-wife, Veronica. He just hoped she was on her best behavior tonight. He'd known Veronica since college, and her vindictive ways hadn't, and probably wouldn't ever change.

"Hello, Veronica," Steven said, turning slowly around. He glanced at Megan, who remained her poised self.

"Oh, Steven, it's a pleasure to see you here. I had a feeling you would be here to support the manatees this year. And who is this lovely *young* girl?"

"This is Megan Chase, my girlfriend. Megan, this is Veronica Scott, my ex-wife."

Veronica's dark eyes stayed on Steven when she addressed Megan.

"Actually, love, it's Dr. Scott-Monroe. I never dropped his last name. I love the way it sounds."

"Nice to meet you, Veronica," Megan said nodding her head instead of shaking her hand.

"Steven, we must do lunch while you're in town. I'm no longer in Fairfax. I just bought a charming brownstone in Georgetown." Veronica turned her back completely to Megan. "Kind of like the one you bought when we first got married. That seems like eons ago, does it not Steven?"

"Still at Georgetown?" Steven said, walking around Veronica to stand next to Megan and wrapping his arm around her waist, pulling her close to him.

"Oh, yes, I simply love being there. After I got my doctorate from Cornell, I applied at Georgetown and a few other colleges. But you know I love D.C. Are you still in college, my dear?" Veronica's gaze finally came to rest on Megan.

"No. I've already finished my bachelor's and master's degrees." Her voice was calm and steady. Steven was pleased. Some of the women he'd dated who had the displeasure of meeting Veronica were always tongued-tied around her.

"Megan has her own interior-design company in Atlanta. She decorates homes for celebrities and other public figures," Steven said, squeezing her even closer and then placing a sweet kiss on her forehead. She tenderly smiled back at him just as Mrs. Douglas had mentioned.

"Oh, how cute. Is that how you two met? Well, I must run. I'm here with Judge Hill, and you know he's the jealous type. Call me about lunch." Veronica strutted away.

"We'll look forward to it," Steven said, calling after her.

"Well, that went well," Megan said, withdrawing herself from his embrace but placing her hand in his as they headed out the door.

"I hope Veronica wasn't too mean. She can be a real witch sometimes."

"No, really?" Megan said sarcastically with a laugh.

"You handled yourself pretty well. Most of the women that I've dated that have met Veronica usually freeze up."

"Well, I'm not most women. Besides, I didn't feel threatened. I'm not really your girlfriend remember?"

"Oh, yeah. I almost forgot."

He hoped she would just forget, as well.

* * *

They rode in silence back to the brownstone. Overall, Megan did have a nice evening. She met some potential clients with a summer place in the Hamptons and was able to give to a charity.

Her thoughts wandered to Veronica and how exotically beautiful she was. Her waist-length natural curly hair was a jet black that brought out her dark, slanted eyes. Her skin was tanned and smooth and her makeup was flawless. She was tall and slender and could pass for a supermodel. Her diamond choker with matching earrings sparkled. Megan could tell she wasn't dolled up for the evening— that was how she always looked.

The more Megan thought about all of the women in Steven's life before her, the more she realized they were all beautiful, high maintenance women who could walk the runways during fashion week in New York or Paris. Sighing, she knew he could never fall for her.

When they arrived back to the brownstone, Megan noticed that the light in Greta's room was on. It was nearly ten o'clock. She had figured Greta would be asleep by now.

"I guess Greta waits up for you?" Megan inquired when the garage door lowered behind them.

"No, not really. She likes you and probably wants to know how your evening went."

"I like her, too," she said, getting out of the car while Steven tossed something in the trash. "She reminds me of my grandmother who passed about five years ago." Megan waited by the door that led to the keeping room.

"Greta is a wonderful person. I really don't need a housekeeper, but I like having her around." He paused. "Well, I'm off to the study to do some work. Thank you for a great evening." Steven fumbled with his keys.

"Work? Do you ever relax? Take a break?" Megan offered.

"No. Then I wouldn't be where I am today. Jeez. I sound like my dad," Steven said, still looking at the keys.

"Do you need some help finding the right key?"

"Um…no. They're just…twisted," he said, still rummaging through them. "You know, it's only around ten on a Saturday night in Washington. How about we go out dancing or something fun? I know of a really cool place. I can teach you how to go-go dance."

"Well, if you don't count a fourth-grade field trip, this is my first time in Washington, so that sounds like fun." She finally grabbed the keys from him and opened the door, which happened to be already unlocked.

"Okay, well let's change clothes and get out of here. According to you, I can use some relaxation," Steven said as they walked up the stairs to his bedroom.

"Didn't you relax playing golf? My dad says it's a very relaxing sport," she said, kicking her heels off once they were in the bedroom. They were beginning to hurt her feet. Then, remembering she wasn't at home, Megan immediately gathered the shoes and placed them neatly in the closet. She went into the bathroom and took the hairpins out of her hair. She had asked Keenan to pin her hair so that it would fall after she took the pins out. It fell perfectly with soft curls on her back. She could hear Steven talking from his closet.

"Nope. We stand around and pretend to care about the other person's golf game. We're really trying to find out each other's opinions on current issues, bills that must be passed, who's running for what and when. So you see, Megan, playing golf with the good old boys wasn't relaxing. It's all politics."

"So is this," Megan whispered to herself, looking through the clothes she brought with her. The clothes from Barney's were being shipped back to Atlanta. Luckily, Chelsea told her to keep a few of the dresses just in case they went somewhere unplanned. Megan reached back to undo her zipper when she remembered that Keenan and Greta had zipped and clasped her gown. She wasn't able to unhook the first clasp. Megan knew that it wouldn't be a good idea to call Greta because she would wonder why Steven couldn't undress his own girlfriend.

"Need some help?" Steven asked, startling her. He had changed into black dress slacks and a yellow polo shirt.

"Yes, please. If you wouldn't mind just unhooking the first clasp. I think there may be another one at the end of the zipper." Megan turned around and lifted her hair off her back.

He undid the clasp, and his hands brushed against her bare back when he lowered the zipper. Heat rushed through her as his warm hands touched her skin. She wanted nothing more than to feel his lips where his hands were. That was when Megan remembered she wasn't wearing any panties because she hadn't wanted the line to show through her dress. She turned around immediately to hide her backside, but it was too late. She heard him whisper *wow* and stepped back, as if to admire the view in front of him.

"I'll be ready in ten minutes," she said, quickly pushing him out the closet and closing the door.

"Cute tush," she heard him say through the door.

Ten minutes later they were on their way down to the garage and backing out of the driveway.

"You look lovely tonight. Is that another Chelsea suggestion?" Steven asked. The strapless purple dress was short and hitting her curvy body in the right places.

"Yes, it is. Chelsea does her job well. She's the best fashion stylist and consultant I know."

"I agree. She referred me to an excellent tailor here in D.C. When I win my father's seat, I'll definitely need one here."

Megan looked out the window. He would win the election, move to D.C. and forget all about her. She decided to change the subject.

"You have a very nice car. It's my dream car."

"Really? You want to drive it? I can have some-one drive it back to Atlanta for you. It just sits in the garage for weeks at a time."

"No. Besides, you have to drive something while you're in D.C."

"I have a few other cars that just sit in the garage. I can have the Range Rover sent to D.C. easily."

"No, my SUV is fine." Megan said. She would love to drive the Lexus, but she'd never been a gold digger, and wasn't about to start. She rarely drove her ex-boyfriend's convertible Porsche or his Mer-cedes when they were together. But every now and then, she saw his nurse happily driving the Porsche around Atlanta.

"Well, if you change your mind, let me know."

They arrived at Capital Club about fifteen min-utes later. After giving the valet the keys, Steven took Megan by the hand and they entered the dance club. They found a table in the back and ordered bottled waters. *The atmosphere is sort of young,* she thought as she looked around. It was mostly college students or fresh out-of-college-students. The floor was packed with people doing all types of dances that Megan had never seen in the clubs in Atlanta. The music blared through the speakers. Strobe lights of red and purple flashed on the dance floor. The DJ played a top forty mix.

"Isn't this place kind of young for you?" Megan screamed over the loud music. She thought they were going to a more upscale location for professionals.

"Yeah. I guess you're right. I used to come here

when I was visiting friends. I was in college at the time," Steven screamed back, looking around. "I feel sort of overdressed looking at all these young men wearing baggy jeans."

Megan was getting tired of screaming, but she didn't have a choice.

"Well, I'm still in my twenties, so I feel fine," Megan answered smiling at him.

"Yes, you certainly are fine," he said, smiling back at her with a wink.

Megan thought she heard him but wanted to be sure. "What did you say? I couldn't hear you. It's rather loud in here," she screamed.

"Nothing. I guess this place isn't for talking," he screamed back.

"Well, since we're here, let's see what you can really do, old man," Megan said, pulling him out of the chair and on to the dance floor.

"We'll see about the 'old man' comment. I'm sure I can outdance you any day of the week!" Steven said, as he jokingly started to imitate some old '70s moves, including the robot and the twist.

They danced and laughed for the next hour straight. He taught her how to go-go dance and she taught him the latest moves from Atlanta that he didn't know. Finally, the DJ played a slow song. But before Megan could turn to walk off the dance floor, Steven pulled her close to him. She didn't resist. She was too tired.

Instead, she let him hold her close. She felt as if she had drunk more than just water. Her dance high was coming down, and she relaxed in his arms. His hands slowly caressed her waist and back. His intent gaze rested on her face. He lowered his head down to hers, and she caressed his neck with her hands as her breaths became heavy. With their lips only centimeters apart, a voice in Megan's head said, *Go ahead and kiss him.* Something told Megan it wasn't make-believe anymore, well unless he was a very good actor. When she realized he was lowering his head to kiss her, she didn't turn away.

Steven kissed her softly on the lips, just enough to taste the strawberry lip gloss she had put on over her lipstick. A hint Chelsea had given if she wanted to make her lips more noticeable and luscious. She wanted him to kiss her some more, but this club wasn't the place.

"Let's get out of here," he whispered to her.

"Okay," she said barely above a whisper. As they rushed out of the club holding hands, Megan still felt the warmth of his lips on hers.

They rode in silence back to his brownstone. He continued to hold her hand, rubbing the inside of her palm with one of his fingers. She had too many thoughts in her head about what had just happened between them. She closed her eyes and rested her head back on the seat. She wasn't sure how to handle her emotions.

Once the car was settled in the garage, neither of them spoke. They still sat holding hands. Megan looked straight ahead, but he was looking directly at her. She decided to let him speak first.

"So are you going to slap me now or later?" he asked jokingly.

"Do you want me to slap you?"

"No. I really want to kiss you again," Steven said, moving toward her and running his finger along her lips. Placing his fingers under her chin, he brought her face closer to his and once again kissed her supple lips, slowly. She responded in the same manner taking her time to taste every inch of his mouth. Warm sensations coursed between her thighs as she returned his kisses with the same passion and vigor that he displayed to her. Low moans of pleasure erupted from her as he kissed her even deeper, letting his tongue penetrate the inside of her mouth.

Her hands roamed over his face while one of his hands caressed the center of her back and the other one massaged her neck. He reached in between her legs under the seat to press a button that moved her seat back as far as it would go. He then reached around her and pushed the back of the seat all the way down, his lips never leaving hers as their kissing intensified and the car windows began to slightly fog. She pulled him on top of her, and he stopped the kiss for moment, taking off his shirt and tossing it in the backseat. His lips placed hot kisses on the side of her neck as she explored her fingers along his hard, muscular back. She could feel the pulsating of his erection through his pants.

Her moaning was unrecognizable as he pulled down the top of her dress, exposing her breasts, which hard hardened and yearned for his tongue, mouth and hands to entice them. He popped one nipple into his mouth, circling his tongue around it before gently tugging it with his teeth. She let out a cry of desire as he continued licking and teasing her breasts going back and forth between the two.

"Steven…that feels so damn good. Please, please don't stop."

"Don't worry. I won't." His voice was heavy, filled with passion. "Not until you're completely satisfied."

He captured her lips once more, thrusting and winding his tongue inside of her mouth. Every fiber in her body was ablaze, and she needed whatever he had to offer to put it out. A cold shower wasn't going to do the trick. She craved him. She had desired him for so long. When she wrapped her legs around his trim waist, he stopped for a second and looked into her eyes as if searching for a sign to go ahead.

She kissed him softly at first and then licked her tongue across his bottom lip causing his breathing to stifle. He slid his hand to the hem of her dress and pulled it up to her stomach. His hand lingered on the band of her panties and then pushed them to the side. He circled her clit with his finger as erotic moans emerged from her mouth. He traced his finger down between her folds as his lips kissed the side of her neck. When he inserted a finger into her slick canal, her breathing became irregular as she thrust her hips up to meet his in and out motion. His lips left her neck trailing down her chest and stomach until he was on his knees in front of her. She shook in anticipation of what she wished would come next, and when he replaced his finger with his warm, wet tongue, she almost exploded. He raised her legs up so that her shoes were in the seat and parted her thighs as he twirled his tongue around inflicting pure ecstasy on her.

"Oh, my goodness, Steven…" she said breathlessly, clutching his shoulders.

"You're so damn wet. You're dripping. I'm the reason. Right, baby?"

"Yes…"

"Who?"

"Yes, Steven."

"That's my girl."

He continued darting in and out of her, cupping his hands under her bottom as her hips moved with the same urgency as his tongue. Her emotions and feelings for him welled up as an orgasm slammed through her body with a force that left her weak and vulnerable yet craving for more of him. The moans and cries eliciting from her were foreign and out of her character, but she didn't care. With him she felt carefree. She could let go and be herself with him and that terrified her.

He lifted up and positioned himself over her. The screech of a zipper sounded, and it wasn't hers. And the conversation she had with her mother yesterday popped into her head.

She immediately pushed him away. "No. This is a big mistake, Steven. I can't do this anymore," Megan said, squirming from under him and pushing open the car door. She pulled her dress down, and rushed into the house and up the stairs to the master bedroom. She didn't know what to do. She was ready to return home to Atlanta and back to her normal life. She had been afraid this would happen. He wanted fringe benefits, as well.

Steven sat in the car for a few minutes before going inside to face Megan. He wasn't sure what had just happened. He thought he and Megan were on the same page. The way she kissed him was like no other kiss he had ever experienced. He'd never been the kissing type. Even while married to Veronica, he seldom kissed. But when he first laid eyes on Megan, the first thought that came to mind was how bad he wanted to taste her lips. And now that he had, he wanted to kiss her juicy lips—both sets.

Sighing, he got out of the car. The last thing he wanted her to feel was hurt, because it was never his intent from the beginning.

When he walked into the bedroom, he saw her packing her suitcase. She was shaken and distraught.

"Where are you going?" he asked quietly.

"Home. I have a credit card. I can pay for my own plane ticket," she said, stuffing her things in her suitcase.

"You can't leave now," he said, taking her by the shoulders and turning her around to face him.

"Why? Because you're scared you won't win the nomination? You're scared how the public is going to look at you?" Megan jerked away, going toward the bathroom. He followed her. "I knew this was a big mistake!"

"No. I…" He stopped midsentence. Now he felt bad. He didn't want her to think he was taking advantage of her, he was very much attracted to her. He couldn't believe it. He had found the one woman who could actually change him into a one-woman man, and she didn't even want him.

"I apologize, Megan. I guess it was the music and the atmosphere. Or it could've been the fact that I was holding a very beautiful woman in my arms, who smells and tastes just like strawberries. Please don't go. Not because of how the public may perceive me, but because it's late, and we've had a long day. Just leave in the morning. We'll tell Greta you had an emergency and had to fly back home early. I'll take you to the airport myself." He hoped she would accept his apology.

"I can take a taxi," Megan said, putting her suitcase down.

"I understand if you don't want to do this anymore," he said sincerely although he had the urge to reach out and pull her close to him.

He watched as Megan sat in the leather chair, contemplating her decision.

"No, I made you a promise. You're right, it's late, and the music and atmosphere played a part, as well. New clause—no more dancing."

"It's a deal," he said, and gently shook her hand.

Chapter 8

The following Monday after her Washington, D.C., trip, Megan was back at work and glad to be doing something to keep her mind off of her fantasy life. She needed to concentrate on her own normal life for a change. She had a million things to do before she headed to Hilton Head that summer to work on the project for the Fabulous Living Channel. She also needed to get her mind off of Steven.

She sipped on a cup of coffee Lucy had made for her. It was storming that morning and no one wanted to make a Starbucks run in the rain.

It had to be the dancing, Megan thought to herself as she took another sip. It had been a while since she'd had that much fun with a man, but Steven was just the wrong man at the right time. While she enjoyed the kiss—among other things—they shared in the car, she didn't want to get her emotions involved, only to be disappointed later. She was glad she was able to leave that Sunday morning to fly back home. Steven had arranged for her to fly first-class back to Atlanta.

Megan continued sipping on her coffee as it surprisingly calmed her nerves. She asked Lucy to refill her cup before her meeting. Chelsea was stopping by to finalize plans for her daughter's bedroom, but Megan knew she really wanted the play-by-play of her Washington weekend.

Chelsea arrived promptly at ten for their meeting. She sashayed into Megan's office wearing a pink Chanel suit. Her diamond earrings and matching tennis bracelet seemed as if they would be too much for someone to wear at ten in the morning. However, it was normal for her. Chelsea believed in being ready for any type of occasion at a moment's notice. The sleeveless dress under her suit jacket could easily be a cocktail dress. Her wristlet that she always kept in her bigger purse could easily double for an evening bag.

Chelsea sat in one of the leather wingback chairs in front of Megan's glass desk and shook her head in disapproval at Megan. "What is up with that white peasant-type blouse? That should be in the bag going to the Salvation Army. I'm sure some young college girl could make use of it." Chelsea rested her Prada bag on Megan's desk.

"Good morning to you, too, sunshine. Can I get

you some coffee?" Megan asked with a hint of sarcasm in her voice.

"No. Hot water, please. I have herbal tea bags in my purse," Chelsea stated, taking one of them out and setting it on the desk.

Megan buzzed Lucy to bring a cup of hot water for Chelsea and more coffee for her. *If the next hour is going to be like this, I may need more than just coffee.*

"I love everything you did to Madison's room. I had Julie put the comforter set on this weekend, and it's simply charming. She's going to adore it when she comes home from Vanderbilt this summer. The last thing will be a nice antique chair for her writing desk."

"Julie? What happened to Amanda?" Megan wondered.

"I had to fire her. She almost ruined my hardwood floors by putting bleach in the bucket. Luckily, I caught her pouring a cap into it and was able to stop her from mopping. A good maid is so hard to find!" Chelsea exclaimed, putting her hand on her forehead.

Megan smiled and thought about how Chelsea would have fit in with the senators' wives at dinner on Saturday night. "Well, I wouldn't know anything about that. I can't afford a maid."

"But, darling, you will once you marry Steven. Now, tell me all about your trip." For the next hour Megan told Chelsea about her trip, leaving out the car incident and argument.

Later on that afternoon Tiffani and Sydney joined

Jade and Megan for lunch at the Cheesecake Factory. The rain had finally stopped and the sun was shining brightly as if it had never rained. It had been a few weeks since they'd had lunch together and Megan needed to catch up on happenings in her girls' lives. Plus, Tiffani and Jade really wanted to hear about Megan's life with the senator. And Megan knew that Sydney needed a break from profiling a new case that kept her up most of the night.

Sydney immediately grabbed the bread basket and began buttering a roll. "Ladies, I'm famished. I haven't eaten since dinner last night, which consisted of two chili dogs, three cups of coffee and two doughnuts. Maybe three doughnuts," Sydney added, as the waiter left with their food orders.

"You were at the GBI office?" Jade asked.

"Since noon yesterday," Sydney stated, squeezing a lemon into her water. "This is the first time I've left. I can't talk about the case of course, but I can tell you it's giving me a headache."

Tiffani sighed and shook her head at Syd.

"Your headache probably came from eating two chili dogs. There's no telling what kind of meat was used to make them, and you stopped eating pork years ago. You know that processed meat is just ground up left over parts from pigs, chickens, and cows all mixed into one hot dog." Tiffani was very health conscious after she found out her late husband had high cholesterol. "We really need to be more aware of what we put into our bodies. We should treat our bodies like a temple and take care of them.

Remember, this is the only body we will ever have. Can't sell it and buy another one like a house."

"You know how to spoil a good time," Jade groaned.

Megan chuckled at Jade, who was actually more of a health nut than Tiffani.

"Tiffani, I'm so glad you could make it. I know you have your hands full. Where's my godson?" Megan asked.

"He's with his grandparents," Tiffani answered. "If it wasn't for my parents, I don't know how I could've gotten through this year. They've been wonderful, and so have all of you."

Megan placed her hand on Tiffani's and squeezed it. "That's what family and friends are for. How's your father doing after that car accident a few months ago?"

"His back has been bothering him again, so Alfonso prescribed something for him and told him to take it easy the next few days." Tiffani looked at Megan apologetically as soon as she uttered her ex-boyfriend's name.

"Tiffani!" Sydney exclaimed, and then looked sympathetically at Megan.

"Oh, girl, I'm so sorry. I didn't mean to mention his name in front of you," Tiffani said with a sincere smile.

But Megan didn't care anymore. It felt good to finally be over him.

"Girl, its fine. He was your father's doctor before we started dating," Megan replied.

"Besides, she's dating a Monroe man now. Forget the doctor. Our little Megan has moved up in the world," Jade reminded everyone.

Tiffani, who still looked sympathetically at Megan chimed in. "How was the fund-raiser in Washington? I read in the newspaper that the foundation raised over $300,000 dollars to save the manatees."

"It was nice. The tiramisu was delicious. I think I may order one today with my lunch, along with an espresso," Megan said, looking at her dessert menu and trying to avoid the conversation. Even though she knew it would come up eventually. She handed them the dessert menu. She knew the only reason Tiffani liked coming to the Cheesecake Factory was for the cheesecake.

"Good idea. I'll take some to go. Dad loves it. I'll probably order him something to eat, as well. I just hope he's feeling better. I worry about him," Tiffani said.

"You know, I have had acupuncture done to help with regulating my menstrual cycle. It also helps with other ailments such as back pains," Jade explained, taking out her doctor's business card and handing it to Tiffani.

"I was reading about acupuncture in one of my alternative health books. I prefer holistic approaches as well but, well, you know men. I don't know if my dad would go for it or not. He's old-school and would probably say it's for women. Megan, do you think Steven would do acupuncture if you suggested it?" Tiffani asked.

Megan remained silent for a moment to collect her thoughts. She didn't know if he would or not. She didn't even know his favorite color or if he was left- or right-handed, so she shrugged and said, "He's a man, what do you think?"

The ladies talked some more, and then Sydney suggested that they go look at the cheesecakes on display at the front of the restaurant. Once they were at the cheesecake counter Sydney said, "We haven't spoken since you returned from your trip, sissy. Did you really have a nice time in Washington?"

"Yes and no," Megan whispered.

"Wait a minute. I know that look. You've fallen in love with Steven!"

"No! Perhaps. Yes!" she finally admitted to her sister. "We get along great. He's really a nice, down-to-earth guy. One would think because of his status and his family's wealth that he would be arrogant and cocky, but he isn't. Well sometimes, but only when he's joking about something. He's a very simple and self-efficient guy. He's so different than what's-his-face who acted like he grew up with a silver spoon in his mouth and flaunted his money like it grew on trees."

"Megan, that's all Steven knows. He grew up having money so it doesn't matter to him. Men like your ex want everyone to know they have made it. A show-off. That's why Daddy never cared for him."

"Syd, when I see him, a part of me wants to rip my clothes off and have him throw me against the wall and make me scream his name."

"Up against the wall? Megan, that doesn't sound like you."

"My point exactly, but I can't stop thinking about having sex with him in all kinds of positions. It keeps me up at night."

"Girl, you got it bad. Real bad."

"What should I do?"

"Well, the best advice I can give is to simply follow your heart. You'll know if he's the right man. It's just a gut feeling that a person has when they know that there's no one else who can make them happy." Sydney spoke in a whimsical voice, which was way outside of her character.

"Syd, is there something you need to tell me?" Megan asked smiling, as they walked back to the table.

"No." Sydney shrugged. "Just speaking in general."

The ladies enjoyed the rest of their lunch for the next hour. Tiffani promised to be home by three to relieve her parents, and Sydney had to go back to the bureau. Jade and Megan rode back to the office in Jade's convertible BMW.

"Megan, are you all right? You don't look that well. Did something you ate not agree with you?"

"My stomach is a little queasy. Just a little jet lag, more than likely," Megan answered. The truth was, she was having confusing feelings about Steven, and it was making her sick.

"When we get back to the office, just get into your car and go home. Lucy and I can handle our appointment. You look like you need some rest," Jade stated.

"Thanks. I could use some more sleep. When I got home yesterday, I finished my project boards for Hilton Head and did laundry," Megan answered. *And I was up all night thinking about my so-called love life. Mostly, fantasizing about how many ways to make love to the Steven,* she added in her mind.

"Well, just go home and get some rest. I'm sure being the girlfriend of a politician can be quite busy and exciting," Jade said, as she parked her car in the parking garage.

Megan hugged Jade and then walked to her car. She didn't need anything from her office. She had work at home to catch up on. Anything to get her mind off of Steven. Luckily, he would be in Washington, D.C., until Wednesday, and then he was going to Florida before coming back to Atlanta next week. If she was lucky, he wouldn't call unless she needed to go somewhere with him, and she wasn't sure if she would be up to going anywhere with him anytime soon.

Megan wanted time to reflect and think about the decision she'd made to date him. If she was falling for him, she didn't know how much longer she could keep up with this charade, because the truth was, she was no longer pretending.

Chapter 9

Almost a week had gone by and Megan still hadn't heard from Steven. It was Saturday afternoon, and she was preparing to leave for her godson's birthday party. She wasn't sure if she should call Steven or not. She tried staying busy by going overboard on projects for clients as well as helping her sorority with a community-service project she hadn't originally signed up for.

She hadn't thought too much about him by the end of the week, at least not during the day. But once her head hit the pillow at night, thoughts of him resided until dawn. She saw him on CNN Thursday morning while she was jogging on the treadmill. The bill he was voting on had passed, and a reporter outside of the capitol in Atlanta was interviewing him. Megan could see that he was freshly shaven and had recently gotten a haircut. His dimples were present and his teeth were white and sparkling.

She had picked up her telephone to call him, but quickly decided not to. She had nothing to say. But in a way she sort of missed talking to him. He was very easy to speak with and was usually in good spirits unlike her ex. She used to have to make him listen to her and even then she knew he wasn't really listening at all. He never wanted to know how her day was, what projects she was working on or even the simplest of concerns like how she was feeling. Steven always asked those questions, and he actually meant them.

Well, I don't have time to sit around and worry about Steven, she thought as she tried to wrap KJ's birthday gift. She hated wrapping presents and would have preferred if she could put it in a gift bag. However, KJ was turning five, and her mother told her a long time ago that children like to unwrap their presents not look in a gift bag. Megan was trying to wrap the present as neatly as possible, but then she remembered KJ was going to just rip the paper off anyway. The finished product looked somewhat decent, but she placed it in a gift bag anyway and decorated it with colorful tissue paper.

"That's better," she said to Percy holding the bag up so he could see it. The cat raised a paw at it. She knew that meant he really wanted to play with the dark blue ribbon she tied on the handles.

Megan glanced at the clock and realized if she

didn't get a move on, she would be late to her god-son's birthday party.

Thirty minutes later she was dressed in a yel-low, flowery sundress with matching yellow wedges. Chelsea had insisted this sundress would be perfect for a Saturday afternoon luncheon with the senator. Of course, a five-year-old's birthday party didn't fit into that category, but she really wanted to wear the dress. Megan pulled her thick hair back into a pony-tail. She had been so busy trying to keep her mind off of Steven that she missed her hair appointment on Thursday and had to reschedule.

"Bye, Percy," Megan said, walking to the door with the gift bag in one hand and a grocery bag with homemade potato salad in the other. Megan wasn't much of cook, but she was always praised for her potato salad.

It was Saturday, so she knew traffic would be a little hectic from Atlanta's Buckhead area to the suburbs in Stone Mountain where Tiffani lived. As Megan stepped off of the elevator, she literally ran into a familiar face with the yummy dimples that she immediately wanted to shower with kisses.

"Hello, Megan."

"Steven, what are you doing here?" she asked surprised that he was there. She had just thought about him when she was in the elevator. *Where was he when I thought about him in the shower? That's where he should've popped up.*

"Well, I was in the neighborhood and decided to stop by. No, that's not true. I just wanted to check on you." Steven raked his eyes over her body, settling them on her manicured toes.

"You could've called," Megan, suggested walking past him toward the parking garage.

"I know, but I just got back in town this morning. I've been so busy with meetings all this week. Plus, I wanted to give you some space."

"I see. Well, I have to go to my godson's birthday party. I'm running sort of late. I should be halfway there now," she said, putting her things in the trunk of her black Mustang.

"I thought you had a SUV?"

"I do. This is my weekend car. It was my first car straight out of college. An impulse buy, at least that's what my dad says. Syd has a red one just like it." Megan stood by the driver's door waiting for him to leave, even though she actually preferred to stay and talk to him.

"So Sydney has a SUV like yours, as well?"

"No. She has a motorcycle."

"Really? Bryce has one, too." He paused and looked around as if he wanted to say something else.

"I really need to go," she said even though she didn't want to.

"I guess I should've called first, but I wasn't sure if you were taking my calls after what happened last weekend."

"All is forgotten," she lied. She couldn't get it out of her head.

"I wanted to see if you wanted to hang out today. Grab some lunch or something. I remembered what you said about me needing to relax. I actually have some free time if you can believe that!" Steven said, opening the door for her.

"Really?"

"No, not really, but I am giving myself free time. I feel like I eat, sleep and dream about politics. There's always some bill I need to read over, complaints from constituents and don't get me started with the rumors in the press. Sometimes, I just want to have a normal day without distractions," Steven complained.

"Well, you can come with me to the birthday party if you want. I mean it's a kiddie party with the pony, face painting and the clown, but you can still come. Tiffani won't mind. She'll probably put you to work though," Megan offered, surprising herself.

"Cool. But I don't have a gift," he said, walking around to the passenger side of her car.

"Do you have cash on you?" she asked as she started the car.

"Why you need some gas? I know the gas prices are getting outrageous, which is another issue we're dealing with," he said, shaking his head.

"No, this car is always on full. But Keith Jr. likes money and saves it faithfully in a tin box under his bed."

"Smart young man. It's best to start now. By the time he retires, there won't be any more Social Security, and he'll have to invest in the stock market or some annuities. But even all of that is questionable." Steven looked through his wallet. "Yeah, I have a few twenties to add to his investment portfolio." Steven took out two twenties from his old worn out wallet.

"One twenty will be fine. You can use the other one to buy a new wallet," Megan said.

"I like my old wallet. I have some new ones, but this one is special to me. It belonged to my grandfather," he said, patting it affectionately. "We were very close."

For the rest of the ride, Steven told her about his meetings at the capitol as well as the recent comments about him in the press. People liked the fact that he had settled down with one woman but most importantly, they liked Megan.

"So, how much longer am I supposed to be your girlfriend?" Megan asked wanting it to end soon so she could go back to her normal life and stop thinking she was in love with him.

"You know, I really hadn't thought about that. It's up to you. Why you have your eyes set on someone else? The ex back in the picture?"

"No. I just want to know so I can move on with my life, and I'm sure you want to get your life back to normal with the ladies," Megan said even though she didn't mean it. But she felt once they were no longer "dating" she would be over him.

"I guess we can cross that bridge when we get to that point. I hadn't thought about being without you. I still want to keep in contact with you."

"Of course. We can still stay in contact. You're a really nice guy, Steven." Megan smiled as they turned onto Tiffani's street. Her house was a beautiful two-story, cream-colored stucco in the middle of the cul de sac. There were plenty of cars already parked in the driveway. Megan hated parking on the street. She always feared someone would hit her car and drive away without leaving a note.

"You ready?" she asked once the car was parked.

"Yeah. Who's all here?" Steven asked, looking at all of the cars. "I can't believe there's almost fifteen cars for a child's birthday party."

"Jade and Syd are here. Kids from Keith's playgroup, karate class and cousins," Megan answered, taking her things out of the trunk.

"Great. I love kids."

"Good. I'm in charge of face painting. You can help me with that," Megan suggested as they walked around to the backyard.

"Wow!" Megan exclaimed as she saw the scene before her. There were about two-dozen kids lined up at different stations. Keith Jr. was on a pony with his grandfather holding the reins. There were kids in the moonwalk and the older kids were in the pool. Megan saw Tiffani and Syd grilling hamburgers and Jade was fanning herself on the deck and setting out the paper goods. Megan was surprised that Jade had even bothered to show up. She didn't care much for a lot of little screaming children running around. Megan set her present on the gift table that was overflowing with nicely wrapped boxes and colorful gift bags.

"Megan, Steven, great to see you two. Steven, I'm so happy you came. I didn't know you liked kids' parties," Tiffani smiled, taking the potato salad from Megan and hugging her at the same time. She then turned to Steven and gave him a big hug.

"I need a break from adults," he said, looking around at the children who were playing and running around.

"How is everything going so far?" Megan asked as they walked toward the grill.

Tiffani placed her hand on her forehead and shook her head as her curly ponytail that was sitting on top swung.

"Girl, terrible! My friend who knows how to make balloon animals was supposed to come, but he called an hour ago and said he wouldn't be able to make it. My dad has to do the pony station, which stinks by the way, and my mom is in charge of the moon-walk area. I can't have these kids getting hurt," Tiffani said in a flustered manner. Megan was used to Tiffani always remaining calm under pressure but at the present moment, she understandably couldn't control her frustrations.

"I can do the balloon animals," Steven volunteered.

"Steven, that's wonderful! The station is already set up next to the face painting," Tiffani said, pointing to the two stations by the back of the fence.

"All right, let's get started," Megan said, but she wanted to say hello to the birthday boy first.

"Godmommy!" Keith Jr. screamed as he ran to give Megan a big hug.

"Hey sweetie. Are you having fun?" she asked, picking him up and giving him a tight hug.

"Yes. Who's this man with you? Where's Dr. Alfonso? He always brings his stethoscope for me to play with. Why isn't he with you?" Keith Jr. asked as she put him down. He was no longer the little baby she used to carry around. Megan glanced at Steven who was snickering at the little boy's comment.

"This is Mr. Steven. He's a friend of mine." Megan hoped that would answer the curious child's question. "Remember, I told you that the doctor and I are no longer friends."

"Nice to meet you little fellow," Steven said, shaking the little boy's hand.

"Did you bring me a present?" Keith Jr. asked as his mother walked over to join the conversation.

"KJ, go play. That isn't a nice thing to ask," Tiffani scolded.

Steven reached into his worn wallet and pulled out the crisp twenty dollar bill and handed it to KJ. "As a matter of fact I do, young man. I heard you like to save money."

"Aww...cool," KJ exclaimed admiring the bill. "Thank you, Mr. Steven. I just got a new wallet, so this is going in there right away." He gave Steven a hug before he skipped away.

Tiffani then made an announcement on her megaphone that lunch would be served in thirty minutes. She also reminded her guests that the face painting and balloon stations were open.

For the next thirty minutes Steven made really

cool balloon animals for the children. His station was the most popular next to the pony. Megan watched him as she painted stars and hearts on the little girls' cheeks.

"So, birthday boy, what animal would you like for the great balloon master to make for you?" Steven asked KJ.

"A puppy!" KJ exclaimed jumping up and down.

"Okay, a puppy it is," Steven said as he began to make the puppy out of black and brown balloons. The children sat in awe as Steven twirled the balloons around each other. Sydney walked up behind Megan whose station was now empty.

"I'm surprised to see him here," Sydney whispered.

"Yeah. Me, too, but he stopped by my apartment as I was leaving. When I invited him, I never thought he would actually say yes. I was just being polite," Megan said as she watched Steven make the puppy for Keith Jr. The kids clapped loudly at the finished product and begged Steven to make more animals. He glanced over at Megan and smiled. She clapped her hands and smiled back.

"What was that?" Syd asked observantly.

"What was what?" Megan asked somewhat annoyed.

"The smile he just gave you and the one you gave him back. Megan you forget I'm a profiler. But most importantly, your twin sister. I know all your facial expressions because I have the same ones and usually for the same exact reasons. That smile and stare meant he loves you girl!" Sydney exclaimed.

"Syd, please stop always trying to read other people's minds. He did a good job on making the balloon puppy for KJ and that's why I'm smiling, so please let it go," Megan answered, agitated. She was never good at hiding her expressions from Syd.

"Well, I know what I saw. And I'm glad I saw it," Sydney said as Megan rolled her eyes.

Megan and Sydney walked over to the balloon station once they were done cleaning up the face-painting materials. Sydney picked up a few of the balloons that had popped.

"You did a great job with the kids and the balloons," Sydney said to Steven.

"Thank you. It was one of my duties when I was growing up. I used to entertain my younger siblings and cousins," Steven answered as he placed the unused balloons back into plastic bags.

Just then Tiffani made another announcement that lunch was ready and for the children to walk over to the round tables where Tiffani, her mother and Jade had prepared lunch.

"You know, Tiffani is so organized," Megan said as she watched her friend tell the children where she wanted them to sit. Jade walked around in her high-heeled sandals pouring fruit punch, looking completely out of place and uncomfortable.

"I hope she decides to go back to work now that KJ is going to kindergarten in the fall," Sydney said. "She never wanted to place him in day care, but I know she's running low on the insurance money now."

"Yes, I know. There are some openings at Mom's

school in the fall, and Dad wrote a recommendation letter for her, as well."

"That's good to know. Then KJ could possibly just go to work with her and save on day care."

"Yep. Just like we did when were growing up."

Sydney laughed. "And we hated every minute of it. I'm going to help Jade. She looks so uncomfortable with the children." Sydney said leaving Megan and Steven alone.

Steven leaned against the table and folded his arms across his chest. "You know I went to school with my mother, as well. I enjoyed it. Bryce and Jacqueline not so much. They stayed in trouble."

"Ha. Sounds just like Syd and Braxton. We went to elementary school with my mother and middle school with my dad. He was the assistant principal at the time."

"Jeez. I guess you couldn't wait until high school where you would be free from your parents," Steven said.

"No. My dad's brother, Tiffani's father, was the principal," Megan answered, thinking back to the times when she and Syd were in high school.

"I guess you and Syd had to be on your best behavior all the time," Steven said.

"Please! She stayed in trouble. My dad caught her smoking in the girl's bathroom in eighth grade. He suspended his own child for three days. My mother was livid at him for a week!"

"He suspended his own child? I don't want to meet him! He sounds pretty tough," Steven balked.

"Yes and no. I'm a daddy's girl whereas Syd is a mommy's girl. She said Syd was probably forced to smoke the cigarette. But the truth is she was the one teaching the other girls. Mommy was mad for weeks," Megan remembered. "Are you ready to go eat? Tiffani is serving hamburgers and chicken tenders for the children, but steaks and salmon for the adults. Syd grills the best salmon," Megan boasted about her sister as she grabbed his hand and walked toward the food area set up for the adults. They ate their lunch at the adult-only table. KJ's older cousins were put in charge of the children so the adults could take a break.

After lunch, the children were entertained again with more balloon animals, face painting and swimming. Five of the boys were spending the night, but Tiffani's father was in charge of that. Tiffani had worked hard all week to prepare for the party, and was going to relax for the rest of the evening. Megan and Steven said their goodbyes to everyone after they helped clean up.

"So did you have a nice time?" Megan asked as they were leaving the party.

"I did. Your friends are really nice," Steven said, looking through her CD case.

"You want the top down?" she asked.

"Sure, why not," Steven said, leaning back in his seat and dozing off as the sounds of Corrine Bailey Rae filled the car.

Megan looked over at him as he slept. Even in his sleep he was handsome. She kept thinking about what Syd said. Megan thought they made a nice couple as well, but she knew it was all business. She wasn't one of the fabulous glamour girls he was used to dating. Even though Chelsea had tried to give Megan a new image, she still felt like the same old down-to-earth Megan. She didn't know how she would even fit into his world.

"Wake up, sleepyhead," Megan said softly to him as they pulled into her parking garage.

Steven slowly opened his eyes and turned his head toward her. "Man, I was tired. I guess it has been a long week," Steven said as he stretched his arms and yawned.

"Yes, you were knocked out snoring over there," she teased.

"Snoring? I know I wasn't snoring."

"No, I'm just teasing. Although you were sleeping quite soundly. Perhaps you should go home and get some rest tonight instead of working," Megan suggested.

"As good as that sounds, I have some work to catch up on. I really enjoyed the party though. It was a way to leave my reality at least for a little bit. Thank you for inviting me," Steven said, getting out of the car.

"You want to come up for some coffee? I just bought some Mexican organic coffee I've been wanting to try. It will wake you right up!" Megan asked, not believing that she just asked him to come in for coffee. Men usually thought that was actually an invitation for sex.

"Yeah. That sounds great," Steven said.

When they were settled into the loft, Megan told Steven to make himself comfortable on the couch while she prepared the coffee.

"Nice place. You have it decorated beautifully. It's classy and elegant. Reminds me of you."

"Thank you. I like to come home to calm sur-roundings unlike all of the outrageous things my client's request. I just like to have things around me that mean something to me such as my grandmoth-er's grandfather clock or my lamp I made out of sea shells I found on Pensacola Beach." She sat the cof-fee in front of him on the table and returned to the kitchen.

"It's very eclectic."

"Do you need cream or milk? Megan asked, tak-ing both out of the refrigerator.

"Neither. I like my coffee black and just a little sugar. Anything else and the coffee loses its flavor," Steven answered, blowing the hot coffee.

"I see. Well, I like mine extra sweet with milk. I guess I will try your way eventually," she considered as she poured the milk into her coffee.

"This is delicious. I'm not really a coffee drinker. Only when I need a boost," Steven said.

"Well, I love coffee. I could drink it all day. Actu-ally, sometimes I have, which explains why I'm up all night. Maybe I'm not a night person after all," Megan pondered.

"Yeah, maybe you just drink too much coffee," he said laughing.

"Well, it's hard to give a good thing up," she said.

"I'm beginning to believe that. So maybe you should drink decaf," Steven suggested.

"I'm supposed to. After my surgery a few years ago, I tried giving up caffeine," she said, sitting in the chair opposite him.

"What kind of surgery?"

"Nothing major. I had a benign lump in my breast. The surgeon suggested that I stop my caffeine intake. I did some research on it and a found some articles that agreed with his statement while other research stated it didn't matter. However, at that time I trusted him so of course I stopped drinking coffee with caffeine. Plus, my cousin Bria, who is an allergist, suggested I cut down on my caffeine intake. Only recently did I start again," Megan said as she glanced around the loft for a sign of Percy. She got up and looked under her bed. Sure enough Percy was laying down peeking out from under the dust ruffle.

"Do you like cats?" she asked, carrying the cat into the living area.

"I don't like or dislike them. I prefer dogs though. You can't play catch or go running with a cat, and they're too self-absorbed," he answered, rubbing the cat's head. Percy jumped down from Megan's hold and ran back into her room.

"Well, at least he let you pet him," Megan said, settling back in her chair.

"What made you get a cat?"

"It wasn't intentional. I found him as a kitten in the dumpster behind my office a few years ago. Jade and I heard this crying meow, so we got him out. Luckily, he'd managed to climb onto a bag, but he was very weak. I took him to a vet. Percy was dehydrated and very hungry, but he bounced back in a couple of weeks. I took him in only to find him a home, but grew attached, so I kept him. My ex was being a complete jerk around that time and Percy was a nice comfort."

"Megan, what happened between you and Alfonso, if you don't mind me asking you?" Steven curiously began. "I can't figure out why a man would let you go."

"Well, I don't know exactly. It's kind of hard to answer that question. I thought I was doing everything he wanted me to do. I was supportive and caring. His parents and friends loved me as well as my family and friends loved him except for my dad, that is," Megan began.

Steven walked over to the stainless steel coffeepot and helped himself to more coffee and then with a smirk on his face said, "Your dad isn't going to like anyone you bring home no matter what he does or how nice he is to you. That's how fathers are about their precious little girls, you know."

"You're going to be up all night if you have a second cup of that coffee. I told you it's very strong," Megan said, shaking her head. Men never seemed to listen, she thought.

"I'll be up late working. Now, finish telling me about Mr., I mean excuse me, Dr. Alfonso," Steven corrected sarcastically, settling on the floor beside the unlit fireplace and grabbing some oatmeal cookies Megan had placed on the coffee table.

"Well, everything was fine until right before Christmas the year before last. We started spending less time together. We were always together. Even when he was busy with his work, he would try to make time for me. He is a very popular surgeon here in Atlanta with a lot of patients. A lot of women would refer their friends because they thought he was handsome. So he had plenty of female patients, but that never bothered me. Anyway, around Christmas time we scheduled a trip to go to the Bahamas for a week and to return on Christmas Eve so we could spend Christmas with our families. Well, he had an emergency surgery to perform right before we left, and I went alone. He flew down two days later to meet me there, with a tan by the way. Now, explain to me how he got a tan in Atlanta during the winter time? The man was always bundled up! He hates being cold. Well, two days before we were scheduled to leave, he got an emergency phone call and he flew back to the States to perform yet another emergency surgery. And being little naive me, I believed him. I mean things do come up with his patients all of the time. However, when Alfonso is on vacation Dr. Bobb always covers for him if necessary, and he covers for her," Megan said and then paused.

"So, when did you finally realize that he was probably in the Bahamas the whole time with another woman?"

"Well, when I returned back to the States, of

course he was the first person I called. My car was at the airport. I called him to see if I could come straight to his house, but he didn't answer the phone. So I drove to his house anyway because, well, I did have a key. However, my key was to the front door only. When I pulled up, I remembered that Jade and I had his double doors changed out, and I didn't have the new key. I rang the doorbell and called his phone again. I could hear the phone ringing from inside of the house, but still no answer. I left a note on his door and a voice mail that I was back from the Bahamas," Megan said tired of going over this story again with someone. At least this time she wasn't crying like the time she told Tiffani and Jade.

"So what happened next?"

"Well, the next day he came over about 8:00 in the morning with breakfast and a present. He said he had been out with Curtis who is his best friend and didn't get my note until he returned home at 4:00 a.m. I later found out that Curtis and his family were in Denver, Colorado on a ski trip. He did see Curtis that night, but only to drive him to the airport."

"Interesting," Steven said, stretching out on the floor.

"Yes, very interesting considering whenever Al went out with his friends, he always called me no matter what time of night to come over or sometimes he just showed up at my door. Well, like I said, I was still being Ms. Naive, and I believed him except that his tan was much darker than it was when he left me in the Bahamas. But I didn't question him. We exchanged gifts and had breakfast. I thought surely we were going to make love afterward considering one of the gifts I gave him was a purple sheer night-gown with matching lace panties. Usually, if I gave him a gift like lingerie that meant I was definitely in the mood, but he said let's save it for later. That man had never turned down sex!"

"Megan, I don't know a man that would unless he was on his death bed and even then he would prob-ably ask for a Lewinsky or something," Steven said sarcastically.

Megan laughed at Steven's comment as she walked to the kitchen to pour the rest of the coffee into her mug and turned off the coffeemaker.

"That coffee is going to keep you up all night, Miss Lady," Steven said, teasing her.

"Yes, I know, but that's fine. I have a lot of work to do, as well. I have some drapes to make. But let me finish telling you about Dr. Alfonso. So any-way, a few days went by before I saw him again. We were having lunch at his house, mostly leftover Christmas dinner from my parents' dinner party. I was opening the refrigerator to take out some juice when I noticed a brochure about a medical conven-tion in Chicago on the refrigerator. I asked him about it and he casually said it was in a few months. So I said cool. Just let me know the details so I can rear-range my schedule. Whenever he attended a medical conference I always went. He never had to ask me, it was always understood that I would go because he wanted me to go with him. Well, at first he was silent and then he said that I didn't have to go because it was in March and I was always busy in March with decorating homes for the spring. I still insisted, and he said don't worry about it and quickly changed the subject. Then the doorbell rang."

"It was the girl he was seeing behind your back?" Steven asked, sitting all the way up.

"No, it was Dr. Bobb and her husband. She said they were in the neighborhood and they wanted to drop off Alfonso's gift. Well, he didn't look happy to see them at all and tried to rush them out. I gave Dr. Bobb and her husband a hug and told them to come and sit down in the living room. Alfonso had gotten a call on his cell and went to another room to take it. I asked the Bobbs about their Christmas trip and she said they didn't go anywhere for Christmas. But that they were going to Memphis for New Year's Eve to visit her husband's family and wanted to make sure that Alfonso could return the favor since she was on call for him while he was in the Bahamas. I decided not to mention that he flew to the Bahamas later because of an emergency surgery because obviously, by the way the pieces of the puzzle were fitting together, there wasn't an emergency of any kind. So I simply said we had a lovely time. They left a few minutes later to finish delivering other Christmas gifts," Megan said, taking a break from her long story.

She was trying to shorten it, but she felt that certain details were important. But she remembered a man's attention span wasn't that long, especially when Steven said, "Okay, so when did you confront the pig?"

"I'm getting to that. So later on that evening we were in his study. He was writing out some bills, and I was pretending to proofread a medical article he wrote. I decided to ask him about the medical convention again in Chicago. He said don't worry about it and that he wasn't sure if he was going to go or not anyway. I knew something wasn't right. I stood up and decided it was time for me to leave. In doing so, I straightened up the pillows on his couch. And that is when I found my evidence."

"What? What did you find? An earring that wasn't yours?" Steven questioned sitting up from his comfortable position by the fireplace.

"No, worse. A pair of red panties that weren't mine!"

"Damn! You know that girl left them there on purpose for you to find. If it was earrings he could've lied and said they were his mother's or something like that," Steven said. "Not that I would know," he added sheepishly with shrug.

"Ha. Yeah, right. Anyway, he was stunned to see them and claimed that they must be mine, but I wear a small and those panties looked a lot larger. Plus, I don't own anything red and he knows that. Anyway, he decided to tell me the truth about him and his nurse, Shelia. I had a feeling it was her. She was always trying to be overly nice to me when I stopped by the office to visit him. After an hour of arguing, I walked out thus ending our four year relationship."

"So, he didn't try to stop you or beg for your forgiveness?"

"No. He was relieved. In fact, he wanted to end our relationship anyway to be with her, and they're still together now. She lives in his home that Jade and I decorated for him before the breakup. But I've moved on. Alfonso leaving me just left the door open for the right man to come into my life," Megan answered, taking their empty mugs back into the kitchen.

"I'm so sorry to hear all of this. What a fool he is. You're a very special lady, Megan. I'm sure the right man will come along if you just let him," Steven responded, walking to the kitchen behind her.

"Yes, I know," Megan said, loading the dishwasher and trying to hide her face. She knew if he looked at her now, her facial expression would give away her true feelings for him. She was ready for him to leave so she could be alone with her thoughts.

"Do you need some help? I did drink all of your coffee and eat all of your cookies. The least I can do is clean your kitchen," Steven offered, taking one of the dish towels and wiping down the counter.

"No, Steven. It's getting late. I have bored you enough tonight."

"Are you kicking me out?"

"Yes. If you're going to be our next U.S. senator you need to go home and work on your campaign," Megan said, not really wanting him to go. Although, she felt that they were getting too close again, which was something she didn't want to do. Plus, when he mentioned eating all of her cookies, she had a different type of visual.

"You're right. I didn't realize it was almost ten," he said, walking back to the fireplace to retrieve his car keys and cell phone. Megan watched him. He was indeed the perfect man. Handsome, successful, compassionate and determined. He had all of the qualities that she wanted in a man, but she knew it was pointless to dwell on it. A relationship with him would be out of the question.

"What's wrong?" he asked, interrupting her thoughts.

Megan was startled. She hadn't realized she was staring at him so hard. She smiled and brushed it off. "Oh, nothing. I was deep in thought I guess." She turned away to hide her embarrassment.

"Hey, Meg I'm sorry if I brought up old wounds from the past. I won't mention him again," Steven said, walking toward her.

"Oh, I wasn't thinking about him," she said, walking toward the door to let Steven out. "I'm truly over him now."

"Well, I hope I had something to do with it. I mean I know this isn't a real relationship, but I hope I've brought some sunshine to your life," Steven said with his hand on the doorknob.

"You have. Good night, Mr. Monroe," Megan said smiling and opening the door for him. He lightly gave her a kiss on the forehead and left. Once the door shut, Percy ran out from under the bed and rubbed his body on Megan's legs.

"Percy, what am I doing? I have gone and fallen in love with a man I can never have," Megan said as she picked up the cat. She held Percy close as the tears started to roll down her cheeks.

Chapter 10

It was the Monday morning following KJ's birthday party. Megan, Jade and Lucy sat in their staff meeting going over the upcoming week's agenda. Lucy was finally going on her first assignment with Jade to look for vintage furniture for a client that loved antique dressers and wanted four, one for each of her bedrooms. Megan's mind was wandering during the meeting. On Sunday morning while making coffee, she had decided to try it Steven's way and drink it black with just a little sugar. She'd smiled as she realized he was right. It had in fact retained the flavor.

Megan had picked up the phone to call him but hung up before dialing. She was so used to sharing everything with her ex-boyfriends that it seemed natural to call Steven, but she'd had to remind herself that he wasn't really her boyfriend.

"Megan, are you ignoring me?" Jade asked in her usual sassy tone.

Lucy waved her hand in front of Megan's zoned-out face. "Earth to Megan. Are you there?"

"Oh, ladies, forgive me. I spaced out. What were you saying?" Megan asked remembering where she was.

"Did you want to go the furniture store with us?" Jade asked standing and grabbing her belongings from the table.

"No...I'll be at a client's home all day waiting for and arranging furniture."

"Okay, we'll be back this afternoon."

Moments later, Megan sat at her desk contemplating what she needed to do before she left. Then the phone rang. She glanced at the caller ID and saw it was Steven. She hadn't spoken to him since Saturday night. She took a deep breath and answered the phone, "Chase, Whitmore and Associates, how can I help you?" she asked in a cheery tone.

"Hey, Megan, it's Steven. How are you doing this marvelous Monday morning?"

"I'm fine, Steven. What can I do for you?"

"I just wanted to tell you that I had a nice time with you and your friends on Saturday. KJ is a good kid. I see him being an investment broker or maybe Hugh Heffner the way those little four-year-old girls were crowding around him in the moonwalk. Did you see the one that kissed him on his cheek when she was leaving? That was really cute. I like children. They say and do the darnedest things. Do you want children?" he inquired.

"One day. I have to find the right man first," Megan answered. Even though she felt as if she had found the right man, she knew that soon after he received the nomination, their relationship would be over, and she would be alone again.

"I also wanted to tell you that I'm going out of town tomorrow on the campaign trail this week to help out a friend in another state. Anyway, I'll be back on Saturday morning. If you need anything, just leave a voice mail or text on my cell."

"Will do."

"I was hoping to see you tonight. How about I bring some Thai food over, and we watch movies together, unless you'd rather be alone."

Megan didn't want to be alone, and she was looking forward to seeing him considering he would be gone for the rest of the week. She took a deep breath and said, "That would be nice. Thai food and you, of course, are more than welcome to come over this evening."

"Great. I'll see you later."

The rest of the day passed by slowly as Megan remodeled a dining room and a living room for a client. She was looking forward to Steven coming over that evening, and she could barely concentrate on her job. Once home, Megan changed into a pair of jeans, but then decided to slip on a polo shirtdress and pulled her hair back into a loose ponytail. She vacuumed her hardwood, cleaned the kitchen and hung up all of her clothes that were scattered on the bed. Megan kept glancing at the clock. He'd texted her earlier and said he would be over around seven.

Megan sat on the couch and watched her grandfather clock slowly tick by. A little after the hour, her intercom buzzer sounded.

"Yes?"

"Delivery for Megan Chase," Steven said trying to disguise his voice. A few minutes later he was standing in her living room carrying two big bags of Thai food.

"Wow! Did you bring enough for the whole building?" Megan teased as she took the bags from him and placed them on the island in the kitchen.

"Well, I wasn't sure what you liked so I bought different things we can sample. There's a bottle of wine in that bag. I'll put it in the freezer for a few minutes to chill."

"Great!" Megan exclaimed as placed the takeout boxes on the table and then grabbed plates and wineglasses.

"So, do you have any good DVDs? I see you have about two hundred of them over there."

"Yes, but you've probably seen them all," Megan said crossing the room to read off the titles.

"Baby, I rarely go to the movies. I don't have time. Besides, I prefer to watch movies at home. Do you have any nongirlie movies?"

"Yes. But I don't have any scary movies unless you count Scary Movie one, two and three as scary.

I have a lot of comedies." Megan scanned through her collection.

"Let me see what you have. Comedy movies are my favorite next to suspense and drama. *Crimson Tide* is my all-time favorite," Steven said kneeling down on the floor beside her.

"Well, I don't have that, but how about *Kiss the Girls* with Morgan Freeman? It's a suspense movie. I read the book before the movie came out. I couldn't put it down! However, I was picturing Denzel Washington as Alex Cross not Morgan Freeman. Do you want to watch it?" Megan asked, holding up the DVD.

"You know," Steven said, moving closer to her, "I was just thinking about that."

"Cool. I'll put it in," she said, still looking through her collection of movies trying to ignore the fact that he was so close to her that she could feel his breath on her neck.

"I wasn't referring to the movie," Steven replied. Tossing the DVD case on the floor, he kissed Megan passionately on the lips. Megan responded willingly as he laid her down on the floor next to the DVD stand. Steven kissed her hungrily while reaching his right hand under her dress to feel her thighs. His other hand fiddled with her ponytail. He tossed the scrunchy across the floor and dug his hands into her hair.

Passion surged through her as he kissed her, sinking his tongue deeper into her mouth as muffled moans caught inside her throat. His kisses were like the fairy-tale kisses she had always imagined, but never experienced. Passionate. Erotic. Sensual. When his lips left hers she let out a loud cry as he kissed her on her ears and then her neck. His hand trailed down her body and then back underneath her dress, kneading her thighs. When his hands began to pull down her panties, all her senses rushed back into her head, and she pushed him off of her.

"Wait we can't do this," Megan interrupted before jumping up and running to the bathroom with Steven closely running after. She closed the bathroom door before he could come in. She splashed some water on her face as Steven opened the unlocked door.

"Damn it, Megan! Stop running away from me. From us."

"Steven, this is all wrong. You don't want a real relationship with me. This is just pretend until after the election," Megan cried.

"What? You honestly think that? You mean to tell me you didn't feel anything a minute ago? Or even when we were in Washington? Or, hell, when we first met? I'm tired of pretending. I want a real relationship with you, I want to be with you, Megan Chase," he said standing behind her looking at their reflection in the mirror. He placed his hands on her shoulders, but didn't turn her around. "Don't we look good together? We make the perfect team. I knew we would the minute I laid eyes on you," he whispered into her ear, his lips lightly brushing it. She flinched as his lips touched her. Megan looked at their reflection in the mirror.

"Steven…" She turned around to face him with happy tears filling her eyes.

"I think, my lady, we've done enough talking for one night," he said as his lips came crushing down on hers.

Steven lifted her up in his arms and carried her to the bed laying her down gently on the comforter. He placed his body on top of hers, kissing her gently on the lips, trying to savor every inch of her delicious mouth.

Steven had never felt so intense and passionate about a woman before. He knew this was the woman who he wanted to see as he closed his eyes every night and couldn't wait to wake up to the next morning.

"Can I help you out of your dress?" he asked, sitting up to take off his shirt to bare his smooth rippled chest and abdomen. Megan smiled as she ran her fingers and then lips over his chest twirling her tongue around one of his nipples. While she continued to arouse him further, he quickly lifted the dress off of her, throwing it across the room with his shirt.

"Damn, baby. You're so beautiful," he complimented as he raked his eyes over her fuchsia lace bra and panties. He licked his lips as he pulled her toward him to feel her hot bare skin under him.

Once she was nude, he lifted her off of the bed and guided her against a nearby wall.

"I had a fantasy about you pushing me against

this very wall," she said, unbuckling his belt. "And having your way with me."

A cocky half grin crossed his mouth. "Oh, really?"

She nodded, displaying a sexy, lazy grin, and kissed him lightly on the lips as she removed his belt and unbuttoned his slacks.

"Well…I am…" He paused as he returned the kiss and licked her lips. "Here to make all your fantasies come true, precious."

He turned her away from him and placed her hands on the wall causing her to let out fervent moans of pleasure. "Part your legs."

He began slowly gliding his tongue from the base of her neck down her back until he was at her center. Megan moaned loudly as his tongue licked and drank her womanly juices. He squeezed her butt and then slapped it, sinking a finger into her as she squirmed and pleaded with him.

"Oh, Steven, please don't stop," she yelled out, pressing her head on the wall as he continued to tantalize her insides with his tongue and fingers. His answer to her was putting his fingers in as deeply as possible, causing the first of many orgasms that night.

Her legs, and her balance, became undone as he lowered her to the floor and held her in his arms as he massaged her clit. Her cries of passion and desire shattered across the room. He kissed her damp forehead and rubbed her hair until she came down from her high.

"Do you have protection?" she whispered.

"Be patient, my love, we have all night."

"Can't we just skip the foreplay? I've waited so long to have you, Steven," she begged, putting her hand on his very erect penis and massaging it through his pants.

"My insatiable, little Megan," he whispered with his lips hovering over hers. "You want it right now?"

"Yes," she cried out.

"Right here up against the wall like in your fantasy?"

"Wherever you intend to."

"Oh, I intend to make love to you in every possible position tonight, in every possible place in this loft. If we run out of rooms, we may have to go to my place."

"I think I have some condoms somewhere."

"Are they Magnums?"

"Um…no."

"Then that won't work." He took her hand and placed it directly on his penis that was now fully erect and ready thanks to her pleading. "Don't worry, my love. I came prepared."

"Go get it."

He stood them up, placing her back on the wall. He obeyed, taking a few packs of condoms out of his back pants pocket and held them up much to her delight. He wasn't used to a woman barking orders at him. Smirking, he stared at her exquisite body leaning on the wall and stepped toward her, pulling his pants and boxer shorts down at the same time and stepping out of them. "Let's get one thing straight.

I'm in charge and in control," he said placing a condom over his firm rod.

She gulped with wide eyes as she glanced down and then back up at him with a wicked grin on her face.

"Oh, really?" she asked sarcastically.

"Yes, really," he said as he picked her up by her buttocks as if she were light as a feather and slid her up the wall. She wrapped her legs tightly around his waist, and he immediately entered her, wasting no time with his strong thrusts causing her to scream out his name in ecstasy. He pounded her harder and harder while she dug her nails deeper into his shoulders. He knew he would have scars later on but he didn't care. The warmness and wetness of her made him sink further into her spirit and mind. She was causing him to feel things he'd never felt before, and he wanted to make sure that all of him was in tune with her. The more she cried out his name, the more he gave it all to her.

Megan wrapped her legs and arms tighter around him as he carried her from the wall and placed her on the bed. She stared up at him with loving eyes as he filled her even deeper. They rocked back and forth concentrating on each other intently. He moved her legs around his neck and held her hands to the bed, as he went all the way in and then all the way out. Her hips met his strokes at the same cadence.

As they screamed out together, he felt all of the emotions bottled up in his heart rush out of him. He grabbed hold of her tightly as he panted her name and a few curse words over and over in the crook of her neck. As his breathing slowed down, he lifted his head and kissed her lightly on the lips.

He was satisfied yet ready for round two with her. The room was quiet except for the soft sound of the ceiling fan above. Neither of them spoke and there wasn't any need. Their lovemaking had spoken louder than any words they could have uttered to each other.

An hour later, they were still intertwined together lying on top of the comforter. Megan tried to wrestle away from his hold to grab the blanket at the end of the bed. Steven pulled her closer into his body so that her back was completely pressed against his muscular chest.

"Where are you going?"

"To grab the blanket."

"I'm not keeping you warm enough?"

"You are. I just feel weird lying naked on top of the comforter."

"I want to see and feel your sexy little body next to me," he said and then kissed the base of her neck. She let out a soft sigh at his touch and technique. She could feel the hardness of him urgently bearing against her bottom and then the tear of a condom wrapper.

"I need to be inside of you again, Megan," he heavily urged in her ear causing her to feel a shooting sensation as he dived into her once again. He turned her over on her stomach as he continued long strokes, in and out, making her dig her fingers in the mattress. Each time it was more intense causing her to release shuddering orgasms one after the other.

After the fifth orgasm, Megan was so out of it, she barely knew where she was. All she knew was that the man she loved was making her feel so damn good.

He pulled her up so she was on her knees. He placed his hands on her round bottom to guide her.

"Am I making you feel good, baby?"

"Oh, yes. The best," she truthfully said.

As he came inside of her, she swore she heard a roar of a lion escape him.

Megan fell limp on the bed as he rolled off of her. She could still feel him pulsating through her as she laid on her back staring up at the ceiling trying to catch her breath from their escapade. She could tell by the aching in her legs, she may be sore the next day, but it was well worth it.

He lay next to her on his back with his head turned toward her.

"Do you smoke?" she asked.

"Um…no? Why, do you smoke?"

"No, but if I was to start, this would be the perfect time to," she said laughing.

"I agree," he said, pulling her close to him.

Chapter 11

Megan was floating on cloud nine. She had heard of the expression and was now experiencing it. She'd never been happier in a relationship. Steven was kind, thoughtful and honest. He sent flowers, texts on her cell phone and voice mails when he was away from her. He was still busy, but he always found time for her. Megan was also happy because her dad finally liked someone she brought home. Steven and her dad had already played golf at the golf course in her parent's subdivision, and they were planning a weekend trip to see Tiger Woods play.

One evening, Megan was looking over some swatches at her office. She didn't like to work late at night but she had to prepare for the beach house she was decorating that would be featured on the

Fabulous Living Channel. Jade and Lucy had already left and Steven was in meetings all day. They were supposed to have dinner, but at around 4:00 p.m. he'd called and cancelled. He said that he had a lot of work to catch up on and would be at his office all night. She decided to stay late and catch up on work as well since she would be at a client's home for the rest of the week. After work, she decided she would stop by his office and surprise him with dinner. She knew he wouldn't mind since she'd done it a few times before, much to his enjoyment.

She called one of her favorite places to dine and ordered two dinners to go. She wanted to spend as much time with Steven as she could before she left for Hilton Head in a few days.

Megan parked her SUV next to Steven's Range Rover. She noticed another car in the parking lot that didn't look familiar. She hoped he wasn't in a meeting. It was nine at night. Her goal was to convince him to eat and then follow her back to her place for a little romantic time. She walked around to the front of the building. *The door is unlocked so he must be in a meeting,* she thought. She walked into the empty "showroom," as Shawn called it. Ten cubicles were in the middle of the room. On the walls were the copy machine, faxes, water cooler and the worktables. In the back were Steven's and Shawn's offices, a conference room and break room with a bathroom. Steven would usually hold any meetings in the conference room. So she decided to wait in his office.

As she walked back to his office, she noticed the

door was ajar and the light was on. Megan went to the door and stuck her head in. She saw Veronica sitting in Steven's chair and Steven sitting on the desk facing Veronica with his back to the door. Veronica saw Megan peeking in and smiled sweetly at Steven rubbing her hand on his knee.

"I enjoyed catching up over dinner tonight," Veronica said loudly enough for Megan to hear and rubbing her hand back and forth. "We must do this again real soon."

Megan entered the office.

"Oh, hello dear," Veronica said sweetly to Megan. Steven turned around quickly and stood up. He looked surprised and guilty.

"Hello, Veronica. I didn't know you were in town," Megan stated still remaining poised.

"Yes, Veronica came into town this morning. She's speaking at Atlanta Memorial College for a Women's Day program tomorrow," Steven answered calmly.

"I must run now. I need to read over my speech again." Veronica stood, displaying a very short red dress that was clinging to her figure like a glove. "Thank you for a lovely time tonight. Call me and let me know if you can escort me to the banquet on Saturday. You know I only prefer to have a handsome man on my arm, and Judge Hill is unavailable. But you and I always look good together at black-tie affairs," Veronica said kissing Steven on the cheek. She then turned her tall frame toward Megan.

"Bye, Maggy, It was nice to see you again," Veronica said. She then grabbed her purse off of Steven's desk and sashayed out of the office smiling.

Megan waited until she heard Veronica open and close the front door

"I thought you were here working late?" Megan asked in a composed tone.

"I am. I intend to be here until midnight, if not later. Shawn will be back at ten. We have some things to go over. Is there something wrong?" Steven said sitting down in his chair and looking over some papers on his desk, avoiding eye contact.

Megan felt the anger rising in her, but she decided to remain poised and listen to his side of the story of what she'd just walked in on.

"You cancelled our dinner plans this evening," Megan said. She walked over to where he was sitting and stood over him with her right hand on her hip. "And then had the audacity to have dinner with your ex."

"Megan. I didn't just have dinner with her. The president of Atlanta Memorial College was there as well to persuade me to speak at the Woman's Day ceremony tomorrow," Steven said as he stood up and placed his hands on her waist.

Megan stepped back. She was too upset for him to touch her. She didn't want to lose trust in him, but if he was beginning to act like Alfonso, then she was in the wrong relationship once again.

"Really? Are you speaking at the program?" she inquired.

"Yes. I told her I would attend the opening session in the morning."

"You and Veronica looked really cozy when I came in. Are you also escorting her to the banquet on Saturday?"

"No. What's with all of the questions tonight?"

"You lied to me, Steven."

"I didn't lie to you. She called after I cancelled our dinner plans. It was all business. Veronica means nothing to me." Steven grabbed her hands.

"And I guess I don't either if you can't tell me the truth." Megan stormed out of his office and into the showroom.

"Megan, I don't have time for the jealous girlfriend act. I'm in a very serious time in my life right now," Steven said following after her.

"You know what? I don't have time for the ex-wife act right now either. Steven, I heard the way she was speaking to you!"

"She only did that because you were here. This evening at dinner, she barely spoke to me. She was on her cell phone most of the time. Trust me the only man she is after right now is Judge Hill. He's trying to make it to the Supreme Court one day. You've seen the stories on the news about that. Veronica is all about gaining prestige. I know you realized that when you met her in Washington."

"What if someone got a picture of you at dinner tonight with her? It could be all over Twitter and Facebook by now."

"The dinner was at the president's home. There

was definitely no one there to snap any pictures. It was just an innocent dinner. Trust me, there is nothing going on between Veronica and I."

A thought popped into her mind. "Why was Veronica even here at your office if you had dinner at the president's home?"

"We rode together, and she came inside to use my computer for a work-related issue. That's all."

Megan knew he was telling the truth, but she was still uncomfortable with his ex-wife being in his life, especially one as beautiful and vindictive as Veronica. Megan walked over to Steven and put her head on his chest.

"Our first fight," she said staring up at him. He bent down and kissed her tenderly on the lips.

"Well, I guess we need to do some making up," he said walking her back to his office.

"Here?" she asked surprisingly. "Shawn will be here in about thirty minutes." She said looking around.

"Just real quick," he said, kissing her on the neck.

"Okay. But you're never real quick," she said as he carried her back to his office and laid her down on the couch for their make-up session.

"So are you going to hang out with me and Shawn tonight? I know you have some work in your car. You can use the conference room," Steven suggested once they were done and sitting on the couch in his office.

"No, baby. Just come over when you're finished. You have a key. Besides, I'll still be up working on some sketches for the *Decorator's Dream* project. We can make up again when you come over," Megan said, grabbing her to-go bag off the table. She hadn't eaten since lunch.

"It's a deal. I promise," he said.

Steven didn't come over until two in the morning, but they were both too exhausted to make love again. Instead, they cuddled while Percy watched from his bed. Steven also suggested a possible minivacation when she returned from Hilton Head.

Before Steven left that morning, he reassured her he wasn't going to take Veronica to the banquet.

The rest of his week was full with visiting different colleges in the state to discuss his plans for the continuation of the Hope Scholarship. In addition to some other educational programs beneficial to college students.

According to a pole in the Atlanta Newspaper, Steven was in the lead by 75% as a favorite to run for the U.S. Senate now that his father had officially put the rumors to rest that he was indeed retiring at the end of the year.

Steven decided he would announce his plans to run for the U.S. Senate seat soon, as the primary deadline was approaching. He was happier however, that he no longer had to pretend with Megan. They were an official couple. There was a picture of them in the paper with a caption that read, "Has the senator finally settled down or is this just a publicity stunt?" The article went on to comment on his progress and compared his views with other potential candidates.

After Steven returned from speaking at Atlanta Memorial College, he looked over the itinerary Shawn had left for him for the rest of day. He was supposed to have lunch with his father and Bryce and spend dinner and the rest of the evening with Megan. She was leaving the next morning for Hilton Head, and he wanted to spend as much time with her as possible before she left for a week, possibly longer.

As he sat at his desk, Steven thought about lunch with his dad and brother and knew it wouldn't be pleasant. His father was in town to discuss the upcoming election. Steven checked his watch. It was almost one, and he knew if he didn't leave his office now, he would be late for his lunch meeting at the French Peasant.

Arriving twenty minutes late, Steven saw his father and brother sitting in a booth at the back of the restaurant under a skylight. Mr. Monroe always made sure he was given the best table in any restaurant. The art on the walls was intricately wood-carved flowers. Megan had told him that she had designed a client's dining room to replicate the restaurant. The young couple had their wedding reception there and wanted the same atmosphere in their home. Steven suggested the French Peasant to his father because he knew his dad enjoyed intriguing artwork and would appreciate his son being considerate of him. His father stood up to shake his hand, but Bryce stirred his ice tea with his straw and smirked at Steven.

"Son, you're late. That's not a good trait for a politician. They're watching you all of the time, even when you don't realize it. Don't forget you're a very important man. Have been since the day you were born," Mr. Monroe stated, shaking his hand. Steven sat down and glanced at Bryce who was still smirking. Steven wondered who "they" were while he looked at the menu.

"So, Dad, how's Washington?" Steven asked, hoping to sway the conversation off of him. He really wanted to enjoy a relaxing lunch with his father and brother, although he could sense from Bryce's facial expressions that their father had a lot to say.

"My son's political career is at stake. Let's order. We have a lot to discuss."

Steven glanced at Bryce who continued reading the menu, probably glad the heat wasn't on him for a change.

For the next hour, Mr. Monroe drilled and debated Steven on every issue that would come up during the election. When they were done with lunch and his mock debate, Mr. Monroe sat back in his chair looking proudly at his son.

"You're definitely a Monroe man. You both are. We never let anything stand in our way of getting exactly what we want." He leaned over the table toward his sons and whispered. "If you keep doing what you're doing now, you'll be president one day. Your brother could be the attorney general and, of course, you'll find something for your sister and your old man?"

"Of course, Dad. You're the reason I'm where I

am today," Steven complimented. As much as he hated to admit it, he knew he was just like his father. Ambitious, hardworking and determined not to let anyone get in the way of his destiny.

"So now tell me about this Megan Chase. Do we know her family? I haven't had a chance to do an investigation on her yet because you usually recycle your women quite quickly. But I see she's lasted for a few months now, and the media loves her. Is she part of the Chase family that we met a few years ago at Martha's Vineyard?" Mr. Monroe said during dessert.

"She isn't part of the Chase family we met at the vineyard," Steven said as he added way too much sugar to his coffee. His father was making him slightly nervous with his concern for his relationship with Megan.

"I'm glad you've finally settled down with one girl. I was hoping Shawn and Bryce would talk some sense into you. I know you hadn't planned on re-marrying again, but remember it's up to you and Bryce to carry on the Monroe name, with more boys of course. Our family legacy and heritage has been around for generations and it must continue. Could this girl possibly be the one to help make that happen for you?" Mr. Monroe asked, concerned.

"Dad, I hope so. She's perfect in every way, sort of like Mom. She's supportive, independent and doesn't care about playing games."

"Just checking, son. But you mentioned to me that she had her own business. There's nothing wrong with a career woman, but the wife of a U.S. senator needs to be supportive of you. Her main obligation should be you and your family. I'm not trying to sound like a male chauvinist. Your mother taught school, but it wasn't as demanding as having her own business. We don't need any more problems in this family. You already had one divorce, and you know I did everything possible to keep that quiet. And I can't believe that one is flaunting the Monroe name like she's still part of this family," Mr. Monroe said slamming his fist down on the table causing the fork on his dessert plate to fall to the floor.

"We understand, Dad, but I promise you I know what I'm doing with Megan. She's a wonderful person," Steven said taking the bill from the middle of the table.

"It's not Megan I'm worried about," Mr. Monroe said, looking at his cell phone screen and then turning it around to show Steven.

Chapter 12

Megan exhaled as she finished packing the last-minute items that Chelsea suggested, or rather demanded, that she pack. Chelsea had finally left and Megan was exhausted. She'd spent that entire afternoon trying on different outfits. Chelsea had put together a list of clothes for Megan and Jade to wear on the show and had even faxed it to the producers.

Megan took a long refreshing shower, dressed and waited impatiently for Steven to arrive. She had planned a romantic evening for them. The candles were lit in every area of the loft and she had champagne chilling in the freezer. Her Thai take-out order was on the way. Everything was perfect including her new black lace panty-and-bra set under her short black dress she wore the night she met Steven. He told her she looked stunning that night and wanted to see her in the dress again. Megan wanted to make sure he had something to hold him over until her return from Hilton Head.

Megan placed her suitcases by the door so she would be ready in the morning. Steven was taking her to the airport at five in the morning and afterward dropping Percy off at Tiffani's home.

After the Thai food was delivered, she glanced at the clock. Steven would be there soon, and she was ready to eat. She decided she would nibble on an egg roll but her cell phone ringing interrupted her trek to the kitchen.

"What's up Syd?"

"Hey, Megan," she said uneasily. "You're calm."

Megan's heart stopped. The last time Sydney said that, there was a picture of her and Steven all over internet. "More pictures of me and Steven?"

"Steven, yes. You, no. I just emailed you the link."

Megan grabbed her tablet and clicked on the link, her heart stopping again. "I'll call you back."

She paced back and forth with her tablet in her hand in disbelief. In front of her were pictures of Steven from that morning at the Women's Day Program. One of which was with him and Veronica. There were actually several with him and Veronica posing with the students or guests at the event. However, the one that had both Megan and the media in a frenzy was captioned "Is the senator getting cozy with his ex-wife again?" In the picture, Veronica and Steven were walking and holding hands as she stared back at him with a loving smile on her face. Steven was smiling at her, as well.

The article went on to suggest that while the senator was more than likely running for his father's soon to be empty U.S. Senate seat, were he and his ex-wife making amends and getting back together?

At the sound of the doorbell, Megan's anger propelled even higher because she knew who was on the other side of the door. And he was about to feel her wrath.

"Percy, you may want to hide under the bed, sweetie. Mommy's pissed," she said as she stormed toward the door armed with her tablet. Percy followed orders and darted under the bed.

She swung the door open, and the handsome smile Steven wore faded into a questionable stare.

"What the heck is this?" She shoved the tablet in his hand.

He came in and closed the door, tossing his overnight bag on the floor.

"Humph." Megan glanced down at the bag. "You might as well pick that up because you only have two minutes to explain."

"Megan, there's nothing to explain," he stated calmly. "You knew I was speaking this morning at Atlanta Memorial College. You knew Veronica would be there."

"Yes, but what I didn't know was that there was still something going on between you two. I can't believe I actually believed you last night when there she was rubbing on you and flirting with you in front of me. Now there's a picture of you two hold-ing hands and staring all lovey-dovey at each other." She snatched her tablet out of his hand and pointed to the evidence.

"Baby, I know the picture looks suspect, but we weren't really holding hands. She was pulling me along because I arrived late, and I was going on in five minutes. She was rushing me through the crowd and showing me where to go."

"And the lovey-dovey smiles?"

"We were laughing at the crowd of girls whistling and screaming, 'We love you Senator Monroe' and some other choice words about how fine and hand-some I am. The event was recorded and it clearly shows just what I told you. You're more than wel-come to watch it. It was on the local news station earlier. I have nothing to hide from you."

"You think I'm stupid?"

"No. I think you're making a big deal out of noth-ing. You remember the first pictures that circled the net with us? How I was leaning over and whispering in your ear and you were supposedly staring at me all mesmerized according to the media. When actually I was screaming in your ear because the music was loud, and you were staring up at me to listen better."

Megan sighed and sat on the couch. She closed her eyes and rested her head on the pillow. She didn't know what to believe anymore. She loved Steven, but she was beginning to grow tired of life in the spot-light especially now with this Veronica thing. Even though it was probably innocent, the media didn't perceive it that way. He had come full circle and cleaned up his reputation during the past few months thanks to her but also thanks to his determination.

His scent whiffed in her nose, and she sensed he was kneeling in front of her. She opened her eyes as tears fell from them, and he reached up and wiped them just as more silent ones began to fall.

"I'm not him, Megan. I would never cheat on you or disrespect you. I love you way too much to do that."

He gathered her in his arms and moved to the couch, positioning her on his lap. She laid her head on his chest as he gently rubbed her hair.

"I love you, too, Steven, and I do believe and trust you. I just don't trust Veronica."

"Megan, Veronica isn't interested in me at all. Believe me, she wants Judge Hill. She only invited me to the event at the last minute because she's a friend of the president at Atlanta Memorial College, and she wanted to make a good impression. It was all for show for her. That's it."

"Well, when I walked in yesterday she was all over you…"

"Before you walked in, she wasn't. She always does that whenever she meets whoever I'm dating. She likes to intimidate people."

"Well, she doesn't intimidate me."

"That's my girl," he said planting delicate kisses on her neck and ears. He ran his hand down her side. "I see you're wearing my favorite dress tonight."

"I wanted tonight to be special since I'm leaving in the morning."

"And it will still be special, I promise." He kissed her lightly on the lips. "I smell Thai food."

"Yes, it was delivered right before you arrived." She tried to scoot out of his embrace, but he pulled her closer.

"How about dessert first," he suggested as his sexy, dark gaze rested on her face, and he pulled the hem of her dress up to her thighs.

"That sounds wonderful…" She was interrupted by Steven's cell phone ringing.

"Sorry, babe, I told Shawn to only call if it was absolutely necessary. I'll put it on speaker so I can continue my tongue journey on your body."

"Shawn, what's going on?" Steven asked as he still held on to Megan and ran his finger alongside her face.

"Man, we have a major problem. A reporter just called asking if you were in a relationship with Megan only to clean up your image. I told him of course not, and you two were very much in love."

"Okay, that's true. So what's the problem?" Steven asked as Megan listened intently.

"He also stated he had a reliable source that could state otherwise. This reliable source claims she overheard Megan getting upset on the phone about having to sleep in the same bed as you in D.C."

Megan sat up when she realized who it was. "Susan. She must've heard me say that on the plane. Oh, no! Steven, I'm so sorry."

."That's bull! Why is Susan doing this to me?" Steven said as Megan slid off of his lap with wide eyes. He got up and walked away from her and into the kitchen with the phone still on speaker in his hand.

"Well, apparently her and Bryce were having an affair, but he broke it off with her recently and then fired her yesterday."

"I had no idea about them, but why punish me?"

"Bryce said she's trying to extort money from him. When he refused to give her what she asked for, she threatened to tell the media about what she overheard Megan say that day on the flight. I told the reporter none of that was true and hung up the phone. But you know women. Some of them never forgive or forget. They hold grudges for a long time. Man, try to have a nice evening with Megan. I just wanted you to know so you wouldn't hear it or read about it first from another source. I'll release a statement as soon as it comes out in the news."

Steven pounded his fist on the island in the kitchen. He knew he shouldn't be worried, but he was announcing his candidacy for the U.S. Senate seat in a few days. He shook his head. Megan rubbed his back to console him.

"Baby, don't worry about this. Like Shawn said, she's a female with a grudge who just wants money. We know the truth and that's what matters. Your constituents are more interested in what you can do for them not who you're dating," Megan said, trying to comfort him.

"I guess you know I don't handle stress well."

"I know you don't. However, you have people around you that care about you and have your best interests in mind, especially me. Shawn said he would take care of it, right?"

"Baby, I don't know what I would do without your love and support. I love you so much," Steven said looking into her eyes.

"I love you, too," Megan responded smiling up at him as he picked her up and carried her to the bedroom.

He placed her down on the floor, and she slowly unzipped the side zipper of her dress, letting it fall off of her feet. His eyes raked over her body and then he pulled her to him. His fingers slid down her back, unhooking her bra on the way to her bottom where he pulled her panties down over her heels.

"Leave them on," he whispered in Megan's ear.

"With pleasure, Senator Monroe."

He kissed her softly, twirling his tongue around hers in an unhurried, loving caress. Picking her up again, he carried her to the bed, their lips still on each other. Once on top of her, his kisses became more intense. He kissed her deeply with all of the passion he had in him to prove to her that he needed only her. He hated the thought of ever losing her over something that wasn't true.

"I love you, Megan. You hear me. You're the only woman I've ever loved." He kissed her forehead, the tip of her nose and her lips, which formed a huge smile.

"I love you, too, Steven and would love to show you as soon as you take off your clothes."

He slid off the bed and starting unbuckling his pants. "You're right. Why am I fully clothed, and you're lying there with your sexy self wearing nothing but heels and perfume?"

She giggled. "Hurry up."

He rejoined her, laying his body on top of hers once more and claiming her lips in a seductive kiss.

Megan could feel his erection in between her legs. She wanted to wiggle her hips so he could slip in, but she also wanted to savor tonight since she was leaving in the morning. Instead, she kissed him ferociously on the lips while his hands roamed her smooth body.

She took in his kisses and touches hungrily. She felt the urgency in him as she forced her tongue deeper into his mouth to mingle with his. She wanted him to know that she was all his. Being in his loving arms again made her feel safe and secure.

Megan let out soft moans while he kissed her neck and shoulders before trailing down to her breasts that ached for his caress. When he finally reached her stomach, Megan knew where he was going next. She arched back and let him kiss her inner thighs and then the sweet spot in between that had missed his savory tongue. Megan moaned his name over and over again as his tongue licked her most sensitive spot. Once she climaxed, Steven looked up into her heat-filled eyes and knew she was ready for him to take her.

Steven reached in her nightstand and put on his protection. He grabbed her close to him and flipped them over so she was on top. He guided her down inch by inch until he was buried all the way inside. She breathed out and began to slowly move up and down as his hands clasped her butt and pulled her all the way down on him. Her cries of passion became louder as their rhythm increased with each stroke.

Waves of pleasure crashed through her body as her orgasm erupted, shaking her to the core. He flipped her over as they were still joined together and began to give slow, tantalizing thrusts that caused more sensations to flow through every cell of her body. She wasn't sure how much more she could take as she held on to his shoulders as each thrust from him summoned an erotic moan from her. She began to meet his thrusts pulling him deeper into her heart and soul. Their eyes never strayed from each other's faces as the glow of the candles settled on them. They climaxed together moments later, still kissing and staring at each other intently. He kissed her eyes that were lightly misted with tears.

She giggled. "That tickles."

"You're ticklish everywhere. You even laugh sometimes when I'm kissing your other set of lovely lips."

"Only when you have a five o'clock shadow."

He kissed the tip of her nose. "You're adorable, you know that?"

"And hungry. You wore me out." She slid from

under him, and he repositioned them so that she could place her head on his chest.

"Hmm…whenever we have Thai food we always have dessert first."

"Then we should have Thai food more often. Um…Steven?"

"Yes, babe?"

"Can I take my heels off now?"

He laughed out loud and patted her butt. "Of course, babe, and then let's go eat. You know, I'm really going to miss you."

She kicked her shoes off and kissed his cheek. "I'm going to miss you, too."

He captured her lips and flipped her over on her back.

Chapter 13

"Girl, I am so glad we have a day of rest," Megan said as she and Jade lay out by the pool of the beach house that they were staying in on Hilton Head while decorating the home next door. It was Sunday morning, and the ladies were finally able to relax. They had spent three long days going over the renovations with the crew. On Monday, they were to shop for furniture while the crew finished putting in the new kitchen cabinets and granite counter tops that Megan and Jade had chosen.

Megan was glad for the busy work, though. She hated to admit it, but she needed a break away from her life in Atlanta. With the Veronica situation and then Susan trying to expose Megan's relationship with Steven, she needed a breather. She felt better after Shawn released a statement stating that while Megan did tell Steven she didn't want to sleep in the same bed with him, it was because they'd just began dating and she would feel uncomfortable sleeping next to him so early in the relationship. The media seemed to believe it and some of the reports stated that Megan had moral values and other young ladies should follow suit.

Megan was disappointed when she couldn't be by Steven's side on Friday as he officially announced he was running for the U.S. Senate seat. She was able to speak with him briefly afterward before having to meet with the producers of the show about the progress thus far.

"What do you feel like doing today?" Megan asked.

"Sip on mimosas and eat lobster tails," Jade answered as her and Megan toasted their champagne glasses. "But seriously, let's go have lunch at the restaurant that is catering the food for the show. Those shrimp and grits…"

"…were to die for."

Thirty minutes later, they were dressed in sundresses and headed toward the front door.

"What's all that noise?" Megan asked, grabbing her purse from the foyer table and putting on her shades. She handed Jade her purse and shades, as well.

"I don't know. Is the crew working on the house? I thought we were all off today." Jade shrugged as they walked toward the front door.

Megan opened it and was immediately bombarded with cameras flashing, microphones and tape recorders in her face. All the people were speaking at once saying her name, Steven's name and Veronica's name, but she couldn't understand what they were asking. Jade stood in front of her and shielded her away from the reporters, pushing them back with her hands.

"Stand back," Jade yelled. "Ms. Chase isn't answering any of your questions. Now leave. You're trespassing on private property."

"But we just want to know how she feels about this," a reporter said, handing Jade an Atlanta Newspaper along with a few loose photos.

Jade glanced down at them and then back at the reporters. "She has no comment, and I suggest you leave before I call the police or I take my mace or something else out of my purse," Jade said, unzipping her purse on her arm as the reporters stepped back. She turned around, pushed Megan back into the house, and slammed the door and locked it.

"Oh, my goodness!" Megan screamed. "This is ridiculous. Why are they here asking about those pictures taken at the Women's Day Program? It wasn't that big of a deal." Megan plopped on the couch and raised her knees up to her chin. "If they watch the video, they'll clearly see they weren't holding hands. She was pulling him."

Jade glanced back at the newspaper and then the photos in her hand. She sat next to her best friend and spoke softly. "Megan, this is today's newspaper, and the pictures are from last night." She sighed as she handed Megan the paper.

Megan looked at the picture, and her heart immediately sank. In the picture, Steven and Veronica's arms were wrapped around one another as they spoke to another couple at the banquet that Steven had said he wasn't taking Veronica to.

"That lying bastard!" Megan threw the paper across the room.

"You took the words right out of my mouth."

"He said he wasn't taking her to the banquet. When I spoke to him last night, he said Shawn suggested that he go because he'd just announced his candidacy for the Senate ticket. He said Bryce was picking him up." Megan paced back and forth with tears running down her face. "I'm just so tired of this. Is this what my life has become? Now I have reporters hounding me down out of town looking for a statement!"

"Girl, I'm so sorry. Maybe…he…" Jade comforted, handing Megan a tissue and sitting her back on the couch.

Megan shook her head and dried her eyes but more tears came rushing down. "No…this is too much. Apparently, something is still going on with them. The first time…I let it slide, but this is different. He said he wasn't taking her. Heck, he wasn't even going and now that I'm out of town, he decided to take her!"

Megan's phone began to ring from inside of her purse. She knew it was Steven because of the ringtone.

Megan answered it as calm as possible. "What?"

"Baby, it's not what you think, I promise."

"You sound like a broken record, and I'm going to turn it off right now." Megan pressed the end button on the screen and then turned off her cell phone. She handed Jade the photos from the couch and the newspaper off the floor. "Can you burn these? But I guess it doesn't matter. They're all over the internet."

"Of course. Anything else? A glass a wine? A shoulder to cry on?"

"Both," Megan stammered as the tears began to fall uncontrollably.

Steven rang the doorbell at the beach house and then banged on the door. He'd been calling Megan and even Jade but neither would answer their cell phones. He found out from his cousin Justine exactly where Megan was staying and flew out on his private plane to see her face-to-face.

He rang the doorbell again, and Jade opened the door with a scowl and her hands on her hips.

"What?" she asked with an attitude.

"I need to see Megan."

"Humph. Not today you won't. Now back up so the door won't hit you when I slam it."

Steven was already frustrated, and he didn't need Megan's best friend to instigate.

"I just want to speak to Megan," he said calmly.

"She doesn't want to see you ever again. Now I suggest you…"

"It's okay," Megan said walking into the foyer

and standing next Jade. "I know I told you make him go away, but I need to tell him exactly how I feel."

Jade stepped back and let Steven inside. "Okay, I'll be in the kitchen if you need me." She cut her eyes at Steven before walking out of the room.

Megan walked to the living room and Steven followed her. He hated the situation they were in, but he planned on making it right. He wanted nothing more than to pull her into his arms and comfort her. He hated that her eyes were red and her tear-stained face was swollen from crying. He hated that she'd been crying over something that wasn't even true.

She stood by the window that overlooked the ocean with her back to him. She breathed in deeply before turning around with a glare of anger and a fed-up expression in her eyes. But when she spoke her voice was calm and steady.

"Steven, I've had some time to think this afternoon about our relationship. How we met, how we started to date and why we dated in the first place. I knew you were a playboy. I knew about your ex-wife and your past escapades, but I still fell in love with you despite the mixed reservations that I had. But I can't do this anymore."

Tears started to well in her eyes, and she turned away. He then grabbed her and pulled her toward him to face him.

"What are you saying?" He screamed out, surprised at the hatred in her eyes.

"This is a life I don't want. I'm tired of the reporters, your past women, the time away from you.

I want my life back the way it was. I went to work, I came home, worked on projects, went to lunch, on shopping sprees, the spa with my girlfriends and lousy blind dates. Today just made me realize even more that this is not the lifestyle I want to be a part of."

"Megan, I completely understand, but what you think happened didn't. I wasn't with Veronica last night at the banquet."

"Did you not see the paper today?" she asked, the calm in her voice was now replaced with anger.

"I mean, we weren't at the banquet together. She was there with Judge Hill."

"Humph, well you two looked real close with your arms wrapped around each other laughing and having a great time with some other couple, and I looked at the all of the pictures. I never saw Judge Hill."

"Those were her parents. I was just making polite conversation with them, that's all. Judge Hill arrived late so that's probably why there aren't any pictures of him. I've done nothing wrong except be in the right place at the wrong time."

"Steven, even if what you say is true, I simply can't do this anymore." She turned away from him, facing the window once more.

A lump formed in his throat, and he couldn't breathe. He hesitated to ask his next question in fear of already knowing her answer.

"You don't want to be with me?" he quietly asked standing behind her with his hands positioned to touch her shoulders to turn her to him once more.

But the hurt he was beginning to feel prevented him from stepping closer to her. He'd seen the resentment in her cold stare and heard it even more in her tone.

Steven didn't wait for a verbal answer. Her silence said it all.

Chapter 14

Megan sat on her couch wrapped in her favorite pink throw blanket looking over design boards and paint swatches for a new project. A new builder to the metro Atlanta area was starting five new subdivisions and wanted Megan and Jade to decorate ten model homes. He'd seen their work on *Decorator's Dream* three months prior and knew their style would be perfect for his floor plans.

Lucy was done with her internship and was now officially a member of their decorating staff. Her first assignment was to decorate two of the ten homes for the project with Megan overseeing. Business was better than ever since their official debut on the Fabulous Living Channel. Plus, the fact that Megan was the ex-girlfriend of a famous senator added to the high demand for their business. They were in the process of hiring another decorator as well as looking for a bigger office. Jade and Megan also thought it was time to hire a full-time secretary instead of using an intern to do office work. After many interviews, they settled on a young woman named Corrine, who was the only candidate not starstruck by Megan and Jade.

Megan had thought about Steven during the past few months. It was kind of hard not to, considering wherever she went there were billboards, campaign posters and bumper stickers endorsing his run for the U.S. Senate. She was glad that he'd won the primary and she had watched some of his speeches and debates. He'd called her repeatedly and sent flowers upon her return from Hilton Head, but Megan didn't want to be bothered. At one point, she considered hearing him out and perhaps giving him another chance but changed her mind when saw him hugged up with a model at some event. Apparently, he'd moved on and was back to his previous lifestyle.

When Election Day arrived in November and he'd won the seat, she'd wanted to call him and congratulate him but didn't. However, she was pleasantly surprised that he'd worn the tie she gave to him and couldn't hold back a smile when he looked into the camera, ran his hand down the tie, and winked.

The sound of the doorbell interrupted Megan's thoughts of the type of hardwood floors to select for her next project. She wasn't expecting anyone and the only way to get into her building was by calling her through the intercom system or punching in the code that only a few people knew. At least the reporters wouldn't be at her front door even though some had been waiting for her recently outside of the parking garage and at work to ask questions about her break-up with Steven and his recent win.

Peeking out of the peephole, she was surprised by who was standing on the other side of the door. She reluctantly opened the door halfway as Percy darted into the bedroom.

"How did you get into the building? I changed the code."

Steven cocked his head to the side with an arrogant grin. "I have my resources. May I come in? I promise not to stay long."

Megan inhaled and stepped aside to let him in. She closed the door but didn't take her hand off of the handle. Her heartbeat sped up, and she hoped he couldn't hear it. He looked handsome and refreshed in a burgundy sweater with black slacks perfect for the coolness of Atlanta in November. He smelled divine, and his presence reminded her how much she missed him.

"What can I do for you?" She was amazed at how calm and steady her voice was but she couldn't let it show that she was a nervous wreck inside.

He pulled an envelope out of his pocket and handed it to her. "I'm having my victory party at your brother's restaurant tomorrow evening around eight. I would love for you to come. I know it's last minute. I hadn't planned on having one, but my father insisted so my mother planned it this week."

She glanced at the envelope but didn't open it. She remained silent as he continued.

"I know things didn't end well between us, but you were there for me when I needed you and winning the election kind of sucked when I didn't have the woman I love by my side to celebrate."

"Yes, I saw that you won. Congrats. I guess in the end we both got what we wanted. You're now a U.S. senator, or will be officially once you're sworn in at the beginning of the year. And I have a slew of new clients because I dated you." She turned the handle on the door. "Anything else? I have a lot of work to get back to," she lied. She really needed him to hurry up and leave before she found herself wrapped in his warm embrace. She wasn't sure how much longer she could remain composed.

"I sincerely hope you'll be able to make it to the party. It's just an intimate affair with close family and friends…and it would be nice to see your beautiful face among the crowd. Despite everything, I was always faithful to you, Megan. I love you very much and miss the hell out of you. I know my life isn't the simple, normal, drama-free life that you're used to. I honestly hope one day you'll forgive me for what you think I did. If we never get back together, just know you're the love of my life, and I'll love you until I take my last breath."

He closed the gap between them, and Megan found herself against the door. She wanted to move.

Needed to move. But her feet were glued to the floor and his intoxicating scent and his inviting mouth, prevented her from doing so. He lowered his head and kissed her gently on the lips as an exhaling moan escaped her mouth. Her tongue joined in the seductive dance he bestowed on her. He yanked off the pink blanket she was wrapped in and he placed her hands around his neck as his hands found their way around her waist meshing her body into his. He kissed her fervently as if he couldn't get enough and as if it he was hungry and only she could satisfy his appetite. And then he stopped, and she let out a moan, wondering why on earth he halted their passion.

"I want you to think about everything I said especially the kiss we just shared that told me everything I needed to know."

He kissed her lightly on the forehead and left without another word, closing the door behind him.

Megan somehow made it back to the couch on wobbly legs as tears burned her eyes. She could still feel the warmth of Steven's mouth on hers and smell his woodsy cologne on her clothes. She dropped to the couch, grabbed her cell phone and told Sydney everything that had just happened.

"So, are you going to the party? I can pick you up on the way."

"I don't know and…wait a minute. On the way? Were you invited?"

"Um…" Sydney paused. "Yes, I was invited, but I wasn't sure if I was actually going to go."

"You and Braxton are traitors. Not only is it at his restaurant, you're the one that gave Steven the new access code, aren't you?"

"Yes, but I did it because you've been moping around for the last three months, burying yourself in work. When you broke up with what's-his-name, you didn't mope and while you buried yourself in your work, you didn't become a hermit. Bryce said Steven's been moody and didn't even care if he won the election or not. He didn't even want a celebration party."

Megan replayed her sister's words in her head. "Bryce said? I thought you couldn't stand Bryce. Called him an ass if I remember correctly."

"He is an ass, but I ran into him at the federal building, and he told me how much Steven missed you and that he hated how things ended. I never believed anything was going on with him and Veronica. Besides, she's engaged to Judge Hill now."

"Sydney, it's not that easy. I…"

"Do you still love him? That's the question you need to ask yourself. Can you go on with your life without him in it?"

The next evening, Megan sat on her couch changing channels and flipping through a home magazine. She finally settled on the evening news to see what the weather would be like next week since one of her projects included an outdoor living and dining area.

Megan waited for the weather segment to come on by putting the television on mute. She continued perusing through the magazine placing stickies on the items she liked. Percy jumped on the couch causing the remote to fall to the floor and the volume went back up. She heard a very familiar deep voice on the television. It belonged to Senator Steven Monroe. He was touring an after-school program with the news anchor. He looked debonair in one of the tailored suits that Chelsea had most likely suggested for him. He was also wearing the tie that Megan had given him again. The news anchor even commented on the tie stating that it looked like the one he wore on Election Day. With a sincere smile, Steven replied, "This tie is very special to me because of who it's from, and I'll cherish it always."

His statement reminded her of the first time she saw his worn wallet that had belonged to his grandfather, and Steven carried it all the time. She flipped the television off, kissed Percy on the head and ran to her closet taking the rollers out of her hair and throwing her nightgown off in the process.

Less than an hour later, she pulled up to Café Love Jones. She took a deep breath and walked inside of the restaurant. An unfamiliar hostess approached her. Megan knew the entire staff at her brother's restaurant.

"Excuse me miss? Are you here for dinner or the private party on the mezzanine?"

Megan glanced at the staircase that was roped off and had a huge bodyguard standing next to it. One of Steven's campaign posters was on an easel.

"The private party for Steven Monroe."

"May I see your invitation please?" the young hostess said with her hand held out.

"Oh...I don't have it but..."

"Then you can't get in."

Megan had to stop herself from laughing. "I'm the owner's sister."

"Sweetie, three ladies just left here saying the same exact thing. I get it. Senator Monroe is once again Atlanta's most eligible bachelor, but it's a private party for family and friends only. So unless you have an invitation, you aren't getting in."

"Look, I can go anywhere I want to in this restaurant and right now I need to get upstairs. So I suggest you tell big bad wolf over there to move so I can get by." Megan was not about to let anything or anyone stand in the way of her mission.

"What's going on?" Braxton asked coming from the hallway that led to another private room and looking at Megan and then at the hostess.

"Mr. Chase, this woman is trying to get into Senator Monroe's private party. She's the tenth person I've had to turn away. She lied and said she was your sister."

"She *is* my sister Megan, who was definitely invited to the party." Braxton turned toward the bodyguard. "Rick, please let my sister upstairs."

Rick removed the velvet rope, and Megan gave her big brother a kiss on the cheek before running up the stairs in her four-inch heels.

When she made it to the top, she scanned the room for Steven. She spotted him talking to Bryce at the bar. Steven's back was to her. She glanced around the room and saw Syd, Jade and Tiffani all wearing wide smiles and motioning for her to keep walking. Sydney even mouthed, "Go get your man."

Megan took a deep breath and made her way across the room. Bryce, who was leaning on the bar, saw her first but didn't make eye contact. Instead he kept listening and nodding his head. As she moved closer, Steven stopped talking and chuckled.

"Amarige?" he asked.

She smiled. "Yes, it's the only perfume I wear."

Bryce patted Steven on the back, gave Megan an encouraging smile and left. She moved to where Bryce had stood and stared up at Steven.

"You came."

Megan ran her hand down his familiar tie. "Of course, where else would I be? It's your big night."

"Would you like to dance?" He held out his hand.

She placed her hand in his as he walked her out to the empty dance floor. "I'd love to but didn't we agree not to dance together again because of where it always seems to lead?"

He nodded his head and glided his hands around her waist as he drew her toward him. "Hmm...well, if I remember correctly, we had our very first dance in this same spot followed by a very sensual kiss."

He lowered his head and kissed her gently on the lips. She heard cheers and claps from their family and friends. They both stopped kissing and laughed. But then his facial expression turned serious.

"I've missed you, Megan. I can't spend another

second without you. I've been miserable these past few months."

"Me, too, Steven. I'm sorry I ever doubted you."

He kissed her forehead and lowered to one knee as tears welled in her eyes. The room became silent except for a few "oohs and aahs" from the women.

He took both of her hands and placed them over his heart as she began to tremble with anticipation. "Megan Rochelle Chase, will you please do me the honor of being my wife?"

"Oh, Steven. Yes! Yes, I'll marry you."

He stood and captured her in his arms twirling her around in the air as their friends and family ran out to the dance floor to hug and congratulate them.

Later on that evening after a few rounds of love making, they cuddled in front of her fireplace facing each other. Steven ran his hands through her unruly curls and kissed her softly on the lips.

"I've never been happier in my life than I am right now, babe," Steven said in between tender kisses. "I knew when I met you that you would change my life forever."

"And I knew when I met you, that you would be my perfect candidate for love."

Epilogue

One year later

"What?" Megan asked sarcastically as she sat on the bed in her hotel suite at the Four Seasons Hotel flipping the channels on the television.

Jade, trying not to wrinkle her lavender dress, sat carefully on the bed next to Megan.

"You're getting married in less than an hour, and you're trying to watch TV?"

"Jade, relax," Megan patted her best friend's hand with a smile.

"Relax? My best friend is getting married, and I'm supposed to relax? Tiffani, Sydney! Are you going to help me out?"

Sydney came over, also in a lavender dress, and

sat next to Megan who was still wearing her slip. Her princess wedding gown hung on the door.

"Jade, leave Megan alone even though I'm surprised at her coolness. Tiffani, I remember you were a nervous wreck on your wedding day," Sydney reminded. Tiffani nodded her head as she finished her makeup.

"Yes, I remember my wedding day. I was a nervous wreck because of the rain."

Megan then got up and walked toward her wedding gown.

"Ladies, help me with the gown please. My dad will be in here soon. And for your information, I'm not nervous because I'm marrying the man of my dreams. I've waited a whole year to marry him, and the day has finally arrived. You know so many good things have happened this year and getting married on New Year's Eve makes it all the better," Megan said as Sydney buttoned up her wedding gown. Jade nodded her head in agreement.

"I agree girl. I'm still in shock that we have our own television show now on the Fabulous Living Channel! The first season was awesome!" Jade exclaimed.

"Yeah, it was cool traveling to different cities with you in a motor mansion looking for the best decorated homes and planning my wedding all at the same time."

"Well, season two of *The Best Decorated Homes* starts filming in a few months so don't go get pregnant anytime soon!"

"You're so silly. I do want children, but I want to enjoy my husband first. That sounds so unreal to say, *My husband!* Ladies! I'm getting married!"

Five hours later, Megan and Steven sat at their table at Café Love Jones, kissing each other softly. Braxton was having his annual New Year's Eve party and the newlyweds and their friends went over to the restaurant after the reception.

Megan had never been more ecstatic than she was at that very moment. She had won the heart of the man she'd dreamed of since she was a little girl. Being with him made her realize that she'd never even been in love until she met Steven Monroe almost a year and half ago thanks to her SUV's flat tire.

Megan glanced around the room, and her eyes landed on Sydney and Bryce in a heated debate as usual.

"All our siblings seem to do is get into heated discussions about the law," Megan said, nodding her head in their direction.

Steven turned to glance at them and then back at Megan with a snicker. "Yes, they clearly don't get along, but we're all family now. Speaking of family, we haven't discussed when we want to plan for ours."

"How about we spend the next few years practicing, starting tonight?"

"Perfect. I was thinking the exact same thoughts."

* * * * *

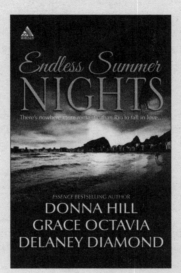

Every passion has a price...

AFTER HOURS

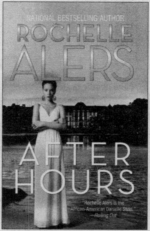

National Bestselling Author

ROCHELLE ALERS

Adina's beauty and wiles have enabled her to adopt the fast-paced lifestyle of the rich and fabulous…until she learns there's a contract out on her life. She flees Brooklyn to start over in an upscale suburb, living among those she's always envied. There she meets Sybil, a secret dominatrix, and Karla, whose need for male attention is spiraling out of control.

As Adina is drawn into the sizzling reality beyond her new friends' perfect facades, she is also hiding her own not-so-innocent past. Now each woman is about to discover that some secrets are simply impossible to keep hidden.

"Fast-paced and well-written."
—RT Book Reviews on *AFTER HOURS*

Available June 2014 wherever books are sold!

REQUEST YOUR FREE BOOKS!

2 FREE NOVELS PLUS 2 FREE GIFTS!

KIMANI™ ROMANCE

Love's ultimate destination!

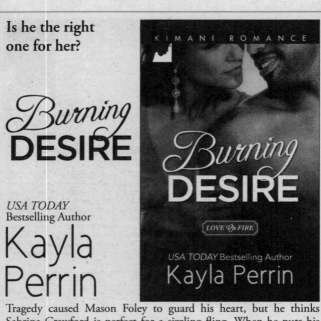

KIMANI ROMANCE

Harmony Evans

Loving LANEY

Harmony Evans

Laney Broward is amazed sh[...]
finally the tabloids have given [...]
heartbreaker Austin Johns. He [...]
but now he will stop at noth[...]
life—and find his way back to [...]

***

THE BROWAR[...]
Passionate [...]

"With endeaving and believable c[...]
life family dra[...]

—[...]